Sailing Through Life In A Rowboat

By Connie L. Hawkins

*Special thanks to my niece,
Danielle Hawkins, whose original
drawing inspired the book cover.*

Registered with The Library of Congress, Washington D.C.

ISBN# 0-9708959-0-9

Sailing Through Life In A Rowboat

To Jay & Gerry Shurlow
who believe in laughter
And to my parents and my Aunt Lill
who believe in me

Acknowledgments

Special thanks to:
Betty Crawford for editing tips
Pastor Josh Quigley from
Bread of Life Worship Center
for the cover design
Danielle Hawkins, whose original drawing became
the inspiration for the book cover
To my family, mostly the inspiration behind this book
My loyal fans and friends
Clip Art-The Print Shop Deluxe; Corel Draw
Photos from the Hawkins' family album
Biblical references The New American Standard Bible
Thomas Nelson-Publishers

Produced by Accent Publications

Contents

Contents

To Margaret,
Happy Sailing!
Connie Hawkins
10-5-10

The Foreword

Sailing Through Life In A Rowboat is a collection of some of the more popular stories and articles by Connie Hawkins that have appeared in various publications over the past 15 years and some new material as well.

The first time I read this manuscript I laughed out loud. The Erma Bombeck of Kawkawlin, Michigan, Connie's cunning wit and dry sense of humor will leave you rolling in the aisles. She doesn't try to be funny, she just is.

Although she told me that she doesn't get along well with kids, her children's stories do not reflect that. She has a natural flare with little people and it comes out in her unique storytelling ability that draws both young and old into her world. *Peter The Reluctant Pumpkin i*s a prime example. Her stories on traveling with young children and camping will make you chuckle. Even when she is serious about her topic, celebrating Halloween for example, you'll be inspired.

It is a pleasure to write this foreword on a very talented author, who in my opinion will go places, just not by car, train or plane! (Read the book). I hope you will enjoy reading *Sailing Through Life In A Rowboat* as much as I did. As Connie says in her introduction, "A merry heart doeth good like a medicine."

Don Stevens
Editor of The Crossroads

Sailing Through Life In A Rowboat

By Connie L. Hawkins

"A merry heart doeth good like medicine."
Proverbs 17:22

In my thirty-plus years as a writer, I've heard, read and written a few articles that have caused more than a chuckle to erupt around the dinner table, amusing anecdotes that I'd like to share in the hope they will bring a smile or two to your lips as well.

It seems fitting that I should write a book like this. After all, the Bible does say in Job 8:11, that "...we should fill our mouths with laughter." It is certainly more pleasing to God than gossip! And is cheaper than drugs and vitamins when it comes to a quick fix for what ails you. Ecclesiastes 3:4, says, "There is a time for everything, a time for tears and a time for laughter," or, as in the case of this book, a time for laughter that will move you to tears.

So good ahead, live a little and laugh a lot--enjoy.

Connie

About the author...

A five-time published author, and past publisher and editor of The Accent Newspaper, Connie lives in Kawkawlin, Michigan (formerly of Linwood) with her husband, Bill, and continues to do freelance work. Although grown now her two children, Heidi and Matthew, still inspire her to write!

Coming...

A must read book for anyone who has ever been involved in building up the temple--or in tearing it down, her next book, *A Teacher, A Preacher, A Music Maker*, the story of a hippie pastor from the West Coast who comes to a conservative town in the Midwest to start a charismatic church premiers soon.

Other publications by Connie Hawkins

Bits and Pieces From My Mind-Four Winds Press 1983
Moments in Love With Jesus-Four Winds Press 1984
Walk Through The World With Me-Self-published 1984
Once Upon A Short Story-Four Winds Press 1987
Numerous articles in The Bay City Times, Tri-City Monthly, The Accent, and The Crossroads.

To find out more about the author, or to order any of Connie's books, please contact:
Accent Publications, P.O. Box 593, Kawkawlin, Michigan 48631 or E-mail connielhawkins@yahoo.com

The perils of sailing in a rowboat

"When I hear complaints that life is hard,
I am always tempted to asked, compared
to what?" Sidney Harris

Talk about a hard life and the perils of sailing on rough seas. I was born with cerebral palsy, and grew up with the label of handicapped. Adults stared, kids taunted. I learned early in life how to row with one oar in the water; the other I used as a weapon for self-defense! Nobody messed with the crippled kid. I knew what it was to have your faith tested. I had the first chapter of James memorized by the time I was eight! Blessed is the man, woman and/ or child who perseveres under trial for great is his reward.

Actually, a sense of humor was my greatest defense against the perils of sailing through life in a rowboat. You've heard that old saying a million times, laugh and the world will laugh with you. Cry and you'll do it alone. No one wants to be around a whiner. Personally, I much prefer to laugh my way through life's blunders. If I didn't, I'd be crying all the time.

Considering I hate anything remotely associated with water (except for relaxing in a hot tub surrounded by tiny bubbles), water walking, skiing, swimming, running through a lawn sprinkler, fishing, and especially boating. I don't understand how it is that I came to sail through life in a half-worn-out rowboat?

Still, God saw fit that I should sail through life. I asked for a yacht--a rowboat is what I got! In spite of stormy waters, life at sea hasn't been too bad. I've had the same shipmate for 28 years. (Five really good years.) My husband likes to think he's the captain of a very tightly run ship. I guess that makes me the first-mate. It's no secret, behind every good man is a woman. Adam had Eve. David had Bathsheba. The president has the First Lady and my husband's got me! Together we've got two excellent deck hands, Heidi and Matthew, both of whom are well skilled in arguing when it comes to whose turn it is to swab the deck.

I've discovered through the years that it doesn't really matter who does what on the boat. The important thing is to keep on rowing --no matter what happens. In my fifty-plus years of living life, I've been up the creek without a paddle many times. Believe me, it's not that much fun to be stuck-a-muck.

I haven't had to worry much about my course in life. God has always made my path known. I have to admit from time to time I have wanted to argue His plan of action, alter life's course, and I still, now and again, complain about the rowboat, but at least it isn't rented (yes, we own it, leaks and all), and at least it will go when you row...*gently down the stream, merrily, merrily, merrily...life is but a dream* or something like that.

"To sail the sea is an occupation at once repulsive and attractive." Hilaire Bellec. How true that is.

Love and romance

"Love is the wisdom of the fool and the
folly of the wise." Samuel Johnson

Have you ever wondered why it takes men so long to fall in love? I knew two weeks after we met that Bill (my husband) was the man I would probably marry. I use the word "probably" because at age 25, marriage wasn't part of my future--not then, anyway.

We dated a year and were engaged several months before we finally took that long walk down the aisle of wedded bliss. Bliss?

I've heard there are five stages of marriage. The honeymoon stage, when everything is wonderful and love abounds. The why did I do it stage, when for the life of you, you can't remember why you married this annoying person. The misery stage. During this stage you can't help but wonder if you're going to make it another year. The settling down stage is the I'm used to him or her now so I might as well stick it out. Finally, 25 years or so later, you hit the "real love" stage. It has to be love--why else would you stay married for 50 years!

Bill and I met in the summer of 1970. There wasn't anything particularly romantic about our meeting, except that we happened to be in the same place at the same time, exchanging a glance across a crowded room. I didn't know where or when, but I knew that we would meet again. And we did.

We started dating. If you can call picnics in the park, popping our own corn for the drive-in movie, window shopping, and a rough ride on the back of a motorcycle, dating. Hey, it was the 70s! And besides, Bill was frugal--nothing has changed.

In December I hinted that we could make beautiful music together. Surely he'd take the suggestion and put a sparkling diamond underneath my Christmas tree, right? Wrong. One thing I learned early on about men--they do not take hints. That year I got an AM-FM radio for Christmas. State of the art.

"It's got duel speakers," Bill was quick to point out when he saw the look of disappointment on my face. "And," he added "it makes beautiful music."

It was spring, my birthday was coming. I told him I could easily picture him a permanent part of my life--what was I thinking?

What did I get for my birthday that year? Guess. A camera, complete with a nylon carrying bag for film. Subtlety does not work with men either, especially Hawkins men!

In June, we had known each other for one year. I had nothing to say. At this point in our relationship, I figured it wouldn't do any good anyway. I'd just have to wait for Bill to realize that he was in love, and he was in love. He just didn't know it!

That's when he said, "I got something for you." And shoved a small, velvet box into my trembling hands.

Sweat started to bead my forehead. My heart began a furious beat, pounding so fast I was sure it would come right through my chest. *This is it,* I thought. The moment I've been dreaming of, waiting 13 long months for, and not so patiently, I might add. I carefully lifted the lid on the delicate box. I couldn't believe it.

"What's this?" I dared to ask.

"It's a Bugs Bunny ring. Do you like it?"

Like wasn't exactly the word I used.

"I don't get it." I was stunned.

"Bugs is my hero," Bill jubilantly explained. (Now, that's sad.) "Everytime you look at Bugs on your pinky--think of me with fondness," he smiled. I, on the other hand, was not smiling.

Oh, I would be thinking of him, that part he had right, but I'm not sure I would be thinking of him with "fondness".

Two weeks later Bill gave me a black pearl, a pre-engagement ring, a promise of things to come. At least it was to my way of thinking. He said he bought it so I'd stop nagging him about that Bugs Bunny ring. I still have that Bugs ring somewhere and the black pearl, too. Every now and then, I like to look at them and remember...what was I thinking, again? I did finally get the real thing, and on a snowy December Saturday in 1972 we were married. The ceremony started late because the groom forgot his shoes! Other than that, the wedding went off without a hitch. The reception was another story however. On the way to the party Bill, trying to help me across the street, slipped on a patch of ice, fell, gashed his knee, tore his pants and injured his pride. Instead of making our way to the reception hall, we were making our way to the five and dime so the bridesmaids could pick up a needle and thread to stitch up Bill's pants! It's a good thing there was a doctor in the house as Bill was in considerable pain and needed an ice pack for his throbbing knee.

That's the year I began writing poetry. I was terrible at it, still am, but Bill said he liked it. Now, that's what I call love. We were supposed to recite the love chapter in the Bible to one another on our wedding day, but Bill got a bad case of the jitters and could barely said "I do." I wrote him a poem:

> When I first met him I called him William
> Then it was Bill
> Later, Billy
> I guess love is like that--isn't it silly?

The poem thing seems pretty lame, now. In fact, I can't believe I am admitting that I wrote it! Worse, I can't believe I'm telling the world I wrote it! (My poetry writing as time went by did improve).

"Love does not consist of gazing at each other, but in looking outward together in the same direction." Antoine De Saint-Exupery.
Now, that is something I wish I had written.

Kids talk about love

"Young men make great mistakes in life; for one
thing they idealize love too much." Benjamin Jowett

I think kids are a great resource when I need help in writing.
So I went to them and asked, *"Hey, kids, what do you know about
love?"* The following is the answers they gave:

I used to think it was chocolate ice cream, and M & M candies,
but now I'm pretty sure love is my cat.
"Are you absolutely sure?"
Pretty sure. When he licks my face with his tongue, it sure
feels like love.

Love is riding my shiny, new bike!

Love is when my mom doesn't yell at my dad because he
forgot to take out the garbage.

Love is taking out the garbage because you love someone.

Love is, hm-m-m...let me think...love is very, very hard to
describe...because you can't see it or feel it really, not like you can
feel the wind...it's like, inside of you, in your heart.

Love is suspecting someone.
"You mean, respecting?"

No, I mean suspecting to do something for someone 'cause you love them.

Love is when you get someone to scratch an itch on your back.

Love is the funny feeling in your stomach.
"Like the kind you get when you go on a ferris wheel?"
Ya, kind of like that, only you don't throw up.

Love is the feeling you get when you're playing with your dog. It's better than playing with your brother!

Love is not rude, dude. I think that's in the Bible. It's one of the Ten Commandments, isn't it?

I think love is saying, "you're sorry" even if you're not.

I don't want to think about love until I'm older.
"How old?"
Maybe around 90.

I love my dad the best.

"Thanks for sharing, kids. I love you."

They all run away. Now, what's that about?

The Gift of love

"Doubt of the reality of love ends by making us doubt everything." Frederick Amiel

December is here again, reminding me of that Christmas when I was nine and found out about Santa Claus. My heart was crushed to think that Santa would be lost to me forever. But then, a miracle happened--a real miracle.

I actually saw the sleigh drive into town that cold December day. A jolly, fat man got out of the sled, dressed in a plaid jacket and pants--both red.

"Are you Santa?" I asked against all hope as I peeked about. "They said you were dead!" I heard myself shout.

"Santa dead?" He said in utter surprise. "Humbug to that!" He shook the snow from his hat. "Come here, Child, sit with me." He climbed back into his sled. I sat on his knee. "Santa Claus," he began, is the love and the happy and most of all, he's the magic that is inside of your heart--and all hearts everywhere. As long as you believe then no one can take the magic away."

"But Uncle said that Santa is not good for religion," in sadness I hung my head.

"Indeed," the old man said. "Why I believe God's greatest gift to mankind is love and love makes me happy. Besides, there's a time for everything."

"Even magic?"

"Exactly and especially," he said.

I smiled for I understood the way only a child could.

"Be good now and always do what's right," he said as I climbed down from the sleigh.

I heard the sleigh bells ring as he drove out of sight. "Happy December," he waved. "See you Christmas Eve night."

Now that I'm grown with babes of my own, I'm still a believer in the love that makes happy and in the magic that dances in two little eyes.

Santa will come. He always has!

Bay City Times - December 22, 1980
The Accent Newspaper - December 1995

What is love?

Scientists don't know what love is, they only know what love does. Love properly applied could virtually empty our asylums, our prisons, our hospitals, wipe out crime. Love is the touchstone of psychiatric treatment. Love can be fostered, extended, used to subjugate hate, cure disease. More and more clearly, every day, out of biology, anthropology, sociology, history, economics, psychology, plain common sense, the necessary mandate of survival--that we love our neighbor as ourselves--is being confirmed and reaffirmed. Christ gave us only one commandment--love. (Author unknown)

The power of love

Life is a hodgepodge of bits and pieces--a little bit of everything, love and laughter, all mixed up.

Life is faith when dreams are lost and hearts are broken, only to be put back together again by the power of love.

From the book *Bits and Pieces From My Mind*
Connie L. Hawkins -1974

The essence of love is, "if"

When I was a little girl I used to ponder the meaning of the word "life", among other things. What is life? I'd asked myself this question over and over. Trying to find the answer to that million dollar question was important to me then and still is.

When I turned 50 I finally figured out what life is.

It's "if."

It's right there between the "i" and the "e"--see it? You have to look closely, but it's there.

The world spends a lot of time eulogizing that word "if." I do it myself.

If only...if maybe...if my parents...if I would have...there's an awful lot hiding between the "i" and the "e".

If we would just concentrate on the essence of life which is love, life would be so much simpler to figure out and problems so much easier to solve.

Sowing seeds of love

I'd like to share the following piece on criticism sent to me by way of a newsletter from a local church.

A little seed lay in the ground and soon began to sprout.
"Now which of all the flowers," it mused, "shall I come out?"
The lily's face is fair and proud, but just a trifle cold.
The rose, I think is rather loud, and then its fashion old.
The violet is very well, but not a flower I'd choose.
Nor yet, the Canterbury bell--I never cared for blues.
And so it criticized each flower, this supercilious seed,
Until it woke one summer hour--and found itself a weed.

I truly hope we as Christians are not like that little seed, that we will take the time to sow seeds of love and kindness wherever we go and in whatever we do!

10

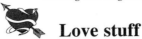 # Love stuff

Valentine's Day, Bah-humbug! As I pushed my way through the throng of last minute card shoppers, I thought, *who needs this?* Who invented all this love stuff, anyway? I'm sure it was some 14th century romanticist or an English poet.

There are numerous stories circulating as to when Valentine's Day actually began. Some authorities trace it to an ancient Roman festival while others connect the idea to saints in the early church. Some link the tradition to an old English belief of birds mating on February 14. The custom of sending a romantic card to your one true love originated in the 1400s, but commercial cards were not printed until the 1800s. Society in general links the "love commitment" to family relationships, and especially stresses the commitment part in marriage.

What was it pastor said about love in one of his sermons? "...love isn't an emotion or even a feeling, it's a choice, an action word. You choose to make a love commitment." Spiritually, God goes one step further when He says, "This is my commandment, that you love one another."

I guess I can put up with a little pushing and shoving on Valentine's Day. After all, a 28 plus year commitment is worth standing in line for a card that says, "I love you...thanks for putting up with me." For those who forget and wait 'til the last minute to buy their sweetheart a card, on V-Day, the stores open early, but keep in mind those heart-shaped romantic cards of endearment go fast. If you're too late for a card, there's always candy, flowers--diamonds! If you can't afford any of the above, consider a homemade gift certificate to sit with the children while your wife gets her hair done, shops, spends an afternoon with friends, or offer to cook dinner. Better yet, take her out! No matter how you chose to say those three little words, "I love you," the important thing is to do it. Maybe all this love stuff isn't so bad after all! Happy Valentine's Day.

The Accent-February 1996

A Sunday school lesson on love

"Love makes everything lovely; hate concentrates itself on one thing, hatred." George McDonald

Susie came home from Sunday school all excited.
"We had a new girl in class today," she told her mother.
"What's her name?"
"Yoko. She's from Japan."
"That's nice," her mother said.
"Some of the kids made fun of her."
"Why would they do that?" Her mother asked.
"Because she looks funny. Her eyes are slanted and her skin is darker than ours."
"What did the teacher do?"
"She baked cookies."
"Cookies?" Susie's mother questioned.
"Gingerbread men," Susie explained. "Some had white frosting on them. Some had chocolate. We all got to taste them."
"Then what happened?"
"They all tasted the same," Susie said. "They were all very, very good. Teacher says that's how God sees us--all the same. All very, very good. She said 'Jesus loves all the children of the world. Red and yellow, black and white, that we are all precious in His sight.' It was our Sunday school lesson."
"What do you think it means?"
"That we should love everyone no matter what color their frosting is!"
As adults we can learn something from this simple, but profound, lesson--to love no matter what--not just on Christmas or Valentine's Day, but every day. In case we forget, God reminds us in I John 4:7, "Beloved, love one another for love is of God."

Bay City Times - February 1992

Love thy neighbor

"Love thy neighbor as thyself." James 2:8

This the story of the Fishmans (a fictitious name, of course). The Fishmans moved into our neighborhood, two or three years ago, maybe longer. Truth is, I can't remember when they moved in.

I do remember I was going to bake some brownies, take them over and properly welcome them to the neighborhood. Mrs. Lensky (also a fictitious name) was going to take over a bouquet of flowers. And so she should; Mrs. Lensky has the most beautiful garden in the neighborhood. My other neighbor (I use the word "other" because I don't know her name) intended to take over a bus schedule, but then decided against it as the Fishmans' son was only 2 months old!

My mother told me in her day when someone new moved in, the whole neighborhood rallied around them. They not only baked brownies, but took fried chicken and potato salad, too! She said, in the old days neighbors did things together. In the summer they had backyard barbecues and picnics. They played cards on cold winter nights and on New Years Eve, everybody brought a dish to share and there was a big party. If there was an illness, well, you did everything you could to help your neighbor. She said, "it was the charitable thing to do--love thy neighbor as thyself. It's in the Bible." Mom says it's too bad that people today don't rally around their neighbors anymore. "You never know when you're going to need the kindness of a good neighbor." I agree with her.

From my window I see Mr. Fishman shoveling his driveway in the winter, and mowing his grass in the summer. The Fishman baby isn't such a baby anymore. It won't be long before they'll need that bus schedule. Mrs. Lensky's flowers, to my knowledge, never made it inside the Fishman's house. Sadly, I never baked those brownies.

I always meant to, but I never did. I'm sorry about that now. I wish I had taken the time to get to know my neighbor.

It's been five years or more since the Fishmans moved into the neighborhood--no one's beat a path to their door. Mother said I should have baked those brownies. What's wrong with me, anyway?

The moral of the story is threefold: One, as the Bible instructs, we should love our neighbors. Two, "Go often to the house of your friend, for weeds choke up the unused path. From *Apples of Gold.* And three, also from *Apples of Gold,* "He who sows kindness reaps friendship, and he who plants kindness gathers love."

We should make every new year a love-gathering year! It's a thought worth considering.

Before I end this story, I want to thank my Linwood neighbor, Dale Hallowell, for plowing out our driveway in the winter. We sincerely appreciated his kindness.

The Accent - January 1996

Out of the mouths of babes

"Kids say the darnedest things." Art Linkletter

I have to agree with Art Linkletter, when he said, that "kids say the darnedest things." He went on to host a successful television show and even wrote a book on the subject. Bill Cosby's 90s TV version of "Kids Say The Darnedest Things," became equally as popular, and that's because kids do say the darnedest things--or is it the "dumbest" things--I forget.

****

Driving home from Grandma's one night, our son, then seven, noticed one lone star up in the sky.

"Wow! Look at that," my husband said. "Only a single star can be seen in the sky tonight."

"That's because God forgot to turn on the other stars," Matthew explained sounding very scientific.

****

Our 10-year old Heidi disappeared one rainy Saturday afternoon. I soon discovered her lying on her bed, arms propped behind her head. "What are you doing?" I asked.

"I'm listening to the rain on the yawnings," she replied.

****

I still remember the Sunday my brother, Stanley, got locked in the Presbyterian Church; he was about four or five. We searched the building high and low, but Little Stanley was nowhere to be found. My mother was frantic. Had someone snatched him away when she wasn't looking? Or, was he simply hiding?

Suddenly we heard kicking and screaming coming from behind closed, locked doors. The pastor ran to the vestibule door and quickly unlocked it. My brother ran sobbing into his arms.

"Stanley, you don't have to be afraid in God's house. Jesus is with you."

"Ya, well I didn't see him," Stanley tearfully sobbed.

My three-year old brother, Bill, wanted a drink of water one day. Too little to climb up on the sink to get it himself, he stood on the floor patiently pointing to the faucet, making little grunting noises as he tried diligently, without success, to get our mother's attention.

"For gosh sakes, Son, if you want a drink, speak!"

Bill's answer. "Woof. Woof."

It worked, he got his drink of water!

****

Heidi was three when we were expecting our second baby. I was relaxing in a hot tub, enjoying a bubble bath when she quietly strolled into the bathroom, her play stethoscope hung around her neck.

"What are you up to?" I asked.

She put a tiny finger to her lips. "Shush..." She quietly whispered as she placed the scope on my swollen tummy, "I'm talking to my brother."

Two months later, Matthew was born.

When we brought him home from the hospital, we weren't sure just how his sister would react to a new baby in the house.

"He's nice," she said, "but I really wanted a sister!" For months she told everyone she saw, "This is my brother, Becky."

Months later, my neighbor called to inform me that Heidi was on her doorstep with her brother in the wagon. Around his neck was a crudely made "for trade" sign.

"I would even take a kitten," she told our neighbor.

She eventually got a kitten. We kept the brother, too.

****

Our daughter wasn't the only one who had trouble with sibling rivalry. A friend of mine said her daughter tried to sell her brother and when that didn't work out, traded him for a sister and a bag of marbles!

"Imagine my shock," she said "when I went into my daughter's room one afternoon and found my neighbor's little baby girl sitting on the floor!"

16

"Don't look so mad," my daughter told me. "I got a good deal. A sister, some jacks and a bag of marbles!"

****

I was still in college when Matthew came along. When he turned three, I enrolled him in the campus daycare program. To prepare him for this exciting new adventure we told him what a big boy he was, that he was going to college with Mom. We bought him a red backpack, filled it with some of his favorite things, and sent him off to daycare while Mom went to class.

At the end of the week he was rewarded for perfect behavior with an ice cream cone at the local dairy. He sat at the table, very grown-up, licking his cone, when an older woman at the next table leaned over and said, "My, but you're a big boy. I bet you go to kindergarten."

"No, ma'am," Matthew replied. "I go to college!"

****

My favorite kid talk story revolves around five-year-old Sally, who loved watermelon, but her mother had to caution her everytime she ate it not to swallow the seeds.

"Why not?" Sally wanted to know.

"Because you'll get fat," her mother, not knowing what else to say, told her. "Now hurry and clean up, we're taking the bus downtown today."

Sally hurried off to wash her hands so they wouldn't miss the bus. They were going shopping. The last stop before the Mall, a very pregnant lady got on the bus and sat across the aisle from Sally, who kept staring which made the woman very uncomfortable.

"Mom, why is that lady so fat?"

"Not now, Dear."

Must have been the watermelon seeds, Sally thought as she continued to stare at the woman's big belly.

"Do I know you?" The woman finally asked.

"No," Sally shook her head, "But I know what you've been doing!"

17

A little traveling music please

"We only need to travel enough to give our intellects an airing." Thoreau

Making travel plans is a major decision at our house. It takes considerable time. No one ever knows where they want to go. Last year I suggested Jamacia. My husband got out the camping equipment and stacked it in the kitchen! Let's get real. Where can a couple go for a romantic holiday with two kids and a cat!

I never know until the last minute where we're going to go, but one thing I do know, I don't want to travel by car to get there. Did you know that automobiles are the cause of 20% of all fatal accidents? So, traveling by car, bus, van or truck is definitely out. Besides, our daughter gets car sick--so does the cat!

I suppose that even though I'm afraid to fly we could go somewhere by plane. Florida's too hot and Arizona, I've heard, averages temperatures over a hundred in the summer. We could fly someplace cool.

We could take a trip by train or boat. A cruise to the Virgin Islands would be ok with me, unless, of course, it's their monsoon season. On second thought, I've been told not to travel by air, rail or water--16% of all accidents are the result of one of these activities.

We could stay home, be it ever so humble, there's no place quite like home. A few years ago we bought a 34-foot 5th-wheel--it cost so much we couldn't afford to take it out of the yard!

Camping in the backyard wasn't too bad. There's boating at the end of our road and the pool is only a few feet away from the back door. At night with your eyes closed, listening to the heavenly sounds of summer--crickets chirping along the ditch bank, the smell of backyard grills smoldering--you'd never know you're not up north.

Staying home is looking pretty good.

The really good thing about staying home (aside from air conditioning in the 5th-wheel, a full living room and galley, master bedroom with his and her closets and a fully operational bathroom-- it's better than our own house) is that when everyone is sawing logs, all snoring in one accord, I can take my blanket, make a mad dash into the house and stretch out in peaceful solitude on a queen-size bed!

Then again, I certainly don't want to stay home. It's a proven fact that 17% of all accidents happen in the home!

And, of course, everybody knows that it's not safe to walk the streets these days. Backpacking, hiking, jogging--any kind of walking is out. Fourteen percent of all accidents happen to pedestrians, usually within two blocks of home.

These are the facts, folks. Having these figures foremost in your mind should make it easier in helping you to decide what to do and how to get where you are going on this year's vacation.

Wait a minute! If my memory serves me correctly, only .001% of all fatal accidents occur in church! There you have it--being in church is the safest place to be on vacation! I wonder if they have room service?

Bay City Times - July 1990

Think before traveling with children

"In America there are two classes of travel--first
class and with children." Robert Benchley

Before you leave on that great American vacation, take a look
at these ten commandments of vacationing. They aren't written in
stone, but they might prove helpful when making travel plans.

1. Thou shalt not leave home without considerable prayer. (I
always pray I won't have to go.)

2. Thou shalt not take the children on every vacation. One
every three to six years is plenty of family togetherness. Children do
not go on vacation to have fun, they go to drive their parents nuts.

3. Thou shalt not leave the driveway without double checking
the oven, the lights, the locks, the garden hose. One year we left the
outside water spigot running. Our son proudly kept this information
to himself for over 100 miles!

4. Thou shalt not position the seat kicker behind the driver; it
will irritate him immensely and make him very angry.

5. Thou shalt not leave home without plenty of aspirin, which
helps thee cope with hysteria when thy daughter casually leans over
the seat and tells you that she thinks she either left the curling iron on
or the shower running--or both!

6. Thou shalt not tell the driver as he's crossing the Michigan/
Indiana border that you forgot to mention the strange noise you heard
coming from the car's engine last week.

7. Thou shalt not mention to anyone over 30 that the extra case
in the trunk contains the family cat. (I was wondering what that scratching
noise was for the last 88 miles) I hope they didn't put the hamster in the
trunk with the cat!

8. Thou shalt not express to these same people that your little brother spilled red pop on the velvet upholstery. Keep it to thyself until the stain dries.

9. Thou shalt not come down with measles, whooping cough, or a fever one day into the vacation. This is against the rules.

10. Thou shalt do all things without grumbling and disputing --because God says so. (Philippians 2:14)

Bay City Times - June 17, 1989

The hazards of summer

"There are many people who prefer to sleep in church.
I don't mean at sermon time in warm weather, but in
the night, and alone." Charles Dickens

Warm or cool, the good 'ole summer time doesn't come without a few hazards, especially for the church.

According to a flyer from Gapway Baptist Church in Lakeland, Florida, low temperatures, overcrowding and sleeping sickness plague the church from June to August.

Low temperatures don't seem to keep most Christians out of the woods. Summer, especially the month of July, brings a frequent and astonishing temperature invasion. Why is it, as soon as the physical temperatures rises, the spiritual one goes down?

Overcrowding is another concern the church faces every summer. The problem occurs mainly on the weekends. However crowded state parks are, there always seems to be plenty of room in the church parking lot. Parks are crowded--churches wish they were.

Sleeping sickness, says Gapway Baptist, is another dangerous distraction of summer. We all suffer from this plague from time to time. I'm not talking about the sickness brought on by the tsetse fly. The sleeping sickness I'm talking about involves the brain and the backbone. Symptoms include: drowsiness and laziness, both usually occur on Sunday morning.

Then, there's the Sunday afternoon coma. I've experienced this one myself. The hot summer weather seems to aggravate this condition. It can actually keep one from attending Sunday evening worship.

Let's not forget midweek amnesia. Local pastors are frantic trying to cope with this one. Most agree that their midweek services have been dramatically affected by midweek amnesia. It must be the warm weather. It definitely seems to bring on a higher incidence of Wednesday night forgetfulness. I don't know about my fellow Christians, but once those temperatures get into the 80s and 90s, it effects my brain! I just can't seem to remember the day or time of midweek service. Wednesday or Thursday, wasn't it?

Let's face it, summer hazards are probably here to stay, but we can do something about them. We all want to see and do all we can on a vacation. It's really in the heat of summer that we realize that "time," as Francis Bacon said, "is the greatest innovator." But unless the appointed time has come, no one, even on vacation, has time to see and do everything. So we might as well take time to see God. In His presence from January to December is always the best place to be. So don't walk, run straight to church.

Camping tests one's Christianity

"I like camping best at home." C. Hawkins

If you really want to test your Christianity, try camping in a 5x6-foot cracker box, more commonly referred to as a pickup camper, with three other people, two of them kids who run in and out all day long, and are constantly fighting over space.

Christ commanded in the Gospel of John to "love one another." At the end of four days (three for me) love goes out the emergency exit. By the time you park the camper in the driveway, you don't even like these people, let alone love them!

Love, according to the guidelines laid down in the book of Corinthians, is supposed to be patient and kind. A weekend of camping in 100 degree temperatures will quickly fry such notions. In humidity, humility takes a hike! At 90 degrees, love becomes irritable, cranky, ill-tempered and downright rude. Whatever happened to "bears all things...endures all things?"

The truth is, at least for me, endurance only goes so far--two and a half days of grinning and bearing it is about all I can muster. When the sweat hits the fan, I knuckle under!

Loving one another is hard enough, but "love thy neighbor..." Now, here is where the true test begins, with neighbors every which way--on top of you, in front, behind and sideways (I thought we came north to get away from it all?)--Screaming kids on scooters, hot wheels and bicycles run wild through the park (you know the place you came for peace and quiet), followed by barking dogs, excited cats, birds and little old ladies in bermuda shorts with frowns on wrinkled brows, speak in scolding tones, chase after the lot of them.

As a mother, I thank God for grandmas. We wouldn't think

of going camping without ours--who'd cook?

Bedtime in a camper is a nightmare! Down go the tables, up go the beds. There are several hurried and tense moments of mass confusion as our teenage daughter tries to decide (while the rest of line up outside the door, anxiously waiting) which nightshirt will look best on her while she sleeps! Or, worse yet, taking what seems like an hour to pick out the shorts and/or bathing suit she'll wear to the beach when tomorrow comes--if it does. She's pushing her luck.

Once everyone has found a spot to lay his weary head--who can sleep? It's too hot. There's not enough air for four people to breathe, consequently my allergies kick in, causing a fit of coughing and sneezing that just won't quit. Overhead bunks are the pits in hot, muggy weather--so two in a bed makes for one uncomfortable night. Maybe we should get a tent with cots! Snoring, three different thundering variations of it, top off a near perfect night (Oh, to have peace). Our house is looking better by the minute. At this point I'd even be glad to see the cat!

The fruits of the Spirit, clearly defined in Galatians, are: love, joy, peace, patience, kindness, self-control...it appears to me, there's been little, if any, of these present this family vacation. It has suddenly occurred to me as Christians we'd have a lot more successful camping trip if, when we packed the grill, the lawn chairs, the bug spray, etc., we wouldn't leave the Holy Spirit home!

Truthfully, as for me, I'd rather write than camp any day.

The Bay City Times - 1989
The Accent Newspaper - 1995

Pats for pets

"Money will buy a pretty good dog, but it won't
buy the wag of his tail." Josh Billings

In Genesis 2:24, God said, "...let the earth bring forth all living creatures." All? I can see the value of a cute little koala bear and giraffes with their long necks are interesting. Birds are nice, too. I've heard tropical fish are very therapeutic and relieve stress, and who among us would deny Flipper his right to exist, but could somebody please explain to me what earthly purpose, or heavenly for that matter, do flies and mosquitoes serve, other than to irritate mankind.

Have you ever wondered why God created cats? I think it was to teach man patience. It's one of the fruits of the Spirit listed in Galatians 5. Our cat tested my patience every day that he was with us. He ambled into our lives in August of 1986. He pompously strutted into the backyard, peering at us cautiously from behind the lilac bush. The kids gave him a bowl of milk. (That was our first mistake.) Next thing I knew, this silver-grey, four-legged feline with mischievous green eyes was slowly edging toward the porch deck. The weather turned cold. Before I could protest, we had a fur ball in the garage--litter box, fuzzy blanket and a ball! That lasted two days.

"Mom, it's cold out, kitty is lonely, can we bring him in the house...please? We'll keep him in the basement. We promise."

From the garage to the basement. From the basement to the kitchen. It wasn't long before our new found friend had the run of the house. It was obvious we had chosen an appropriate name for this cat--King Tut. He ruled the roost with great authority, a true king.

When Tut was good, he was adorable, but when he was bad, he was horrid. The broom, fly swatter and water gun were mere amusements to Tut. He liked them better than balls with bells!

People came from miles to see the infamous Tut cat do tricks. Most amazing was leaping to the top of our 6ft. refrigerator to capture with his paws, mind you, not his teeth, magnets and other little do-dads hanging there. He loved games...chasing after an old jump rope, batting balls round, jumping on your head--that's how he got your attention in the morning when he wanted something to eat! He especially enjoyed scattering leaves. He'd wait until the kids raked them into neat little piles, and then, in a flying hurdle, he'd scatter the debris in every direction.

Truthfully, Tut and I never got along. Ours was a love/hate relationship, that until the end, I didn't realize had grown into something quite special. You see, Tut was no ordinary cat. He loved people. Whereever you were, there he was. I was constantly complaining about that darn cat!

Nine and a half years later, I found myself staring into an empty water dish. The fuzzy blanket, frayed jump rope and balls with bells in them were all gone now--as is King Tut.

Illness forced us to put him to sleep one fall day. It made me realize that death, pet or human, friend or foe, is not easy. It leaves an empty space in your heart. I also realize, thanks to Tut, that patience is a virtue I do have. Pets, like Christ, give unconditional love. We who choose to immerse ourselves in that love are richly blessed.

The Bible says in Ecclesiastics 3, "There is a time for everything under the sun. A time to be born and a time to die. A time to weep, and a time to laugh." Through sorrow, we will have laughter as we remember all the good times we had with a fur ball named King Tut. We'll miss you. Good-bye our fine, furry friend.

King Tut
August 1986-November 1996

From the book
Once Upon A Short Story
By C. Hawkins - 1987
Revised for The Accent -
November 1996

Animals

I think I could turn and live with animals; they are so placid and self-contained. I stand and look at them long and hard. They do not sweat and whine about their condition. They don't lie awake in the dark and weep for their sins.

They do not make me sick discussing their duty to God.

By Walt Whitman

 ## Life on the farm

I wish that I could live on a farm with horses and goats and cows in a barn. With ducks and geese and cats quite tame--ready and waiting for animal games.

What a pity to live in the city and not have one pet to pat.

By Connie Houghtaling-Hawkins, age 10

The vet is all wet

The other day Englehart called. Our church had just finished a cooperative Bible school with his church.

"I've got bad news," Englehart said.

"What is it?" I was almost afraid to ask.

"Missy's got lice."

Missy...my mind was in a whirl. There were at least two Missys in Bible school. "Which one?" I asked.

"The yellow-haired one."

"That's terrible," I lamented. "What am I supposed to do about it?"

"You could fog the house," he said.

"Fog the house. Why? Missy was never in my house."

"She wasn't. Are you sure?"

"Of course, I'm sure. She was at the church with the others."

The others? The registration said there were no others."

"That's impossible," I said. "There were 93 in all."

"Ninety-three!" Englehart shrieked. "That's practically an epidemic. They should all be seen by a doctor."

"I'm horrified," I confessed. "What are we going to tell our friends and neighbors?"

"I don't know what to tell you," Englehart admitted. "Do you still want to go ahead with Missy's surgery?"

"Surgery? What surgery?" I dumbfoundedly asked. Why was he asking me, anyway. Missy wasn't even mine.

"You realize, of course, once she has the surgery, she won't be able to have babies."

"Babies! Isn't she a bit young for that?" Again, I was horrified Missy couldn't be more than 10. And why was Englehart discussing such a personal situation with me? I was after all, only Missy's teacher.

"Babies having babies. It happens all the time," Englehart explained. "Something should be done about it before the earth becomes over populated."

I was appalled. *This is no way for a minister to talk*, I thought to myself.

"There's simply too many animals running around, now," he said.

"Animals?" Suddenly it dawned on me. "You're not Pastor Englehart, are you?"

"No," he said. "This is Dr. Englehart, your vet."

"And Missy is?"

"Your cat, the one you brought in this morning to be neutered."

It took me several long minutes to realize that Englehart was talking about Missy, a stray cat my cousin had taken to his clinic to be fixed so she couldn't have kittens. After the misunderstanding was cleared up we all had a good laugh. I say "all" because I suspect God may have had a chuckle over this one.

Who says God doesn't have a sense of humor?

"Laughing is the sensation of feeling good all over
and showing it principally in one spot." Josh Billings

My mother told me, "God must really have a sense of humor."
"What do you mean?" I had to ask.
"He put you in charge of running a newspaper, didn't he?"
I knew she saw the blooper: "Food panty seeks warehouse"
--that one was a doozy.

Keeping in mind a merry heart doeth good like a medicine, I thought I'd share some media bloopers with you.

Two of my biggest blunders came in issues three and five. In issue three, not only did I misspell the business accent of the month, I gave it a whole new name! Luckily the owner was a good friend of mine. Our photographer interviewed the owner of a bike shop for the business feature in issue five. Imagine her surprise when she opened the paper and read a quote from the owner's wife, who wasn't even present during the interview! We still laugh about that one.

One of the first things I wrote professionally was a wedding review. I was doing great, until the last sentence when I wrote, "the reception was hell at Village Hall." Whoops, the slip of a 'd'.

The following writing assignment in my journalism class warrants a chuckle. "A United Air lines jet with 61 passengers aboard crashed while approaching Chicago's Midway Airport. Most of the survivors were killed when the airliner plowed through homes in the city's residential district..." The survivors were killed? Whoops.

Errors in "gramma" are far too common in newspaper writing, and because of them, meaning is often obscured. Consider the following examples:

Each of the boys brought their sleeping bags.
The mayor agreed to soon submit his resignation.
Despite his size, the coach said Jones would play forward.

They're hard to spot, but we have an incorrect antecedent, a split infinitive and a misplaced modifier, not to mention a misspelled word (grammar) in the lead sentence. All good for a laugh, but a bit embarrassing for the editor of a newspaper.

I like this news article from a budding journalist of a small town publication: *The Browns' prized Irish setter was struck by a car Tuesday afternoon. Killed and left for dead, the Browns were rushed to the vet. Injuries were so severe, the dog was laid to rest.*

The way this article was written makes it sound like the Browns were killed and rushed to the vet. It goes on to state, injuries were so severe the dog was laid to rest (put to sleep). I thought the dog was already dead? If so, why was he rushed to the vet?

I make my share of media blunders. To make life easier, I prefer to think that God does have a sense of humor and that perhaps, He's sitting on a white, fluffy cloud right now, lamenting as he reads this months Accent. Lamenting? Maybe that's the wrong word.

Who says you don't need a sense of humor to run a newspaper?

Complain--who me?

"He who complains, sins." St. Frances DeSales

The world is full of complainers (my mother calls them whiners). It's really nothing new. Mankind has been complaining since the world began. I'm sure it started with Eve--remember the story of the forbidden fruit? Eve wasn't happy being told what she could or could not eat.

And what about Cain and Abel--one brother's complaint against the other led to a tragic end. Job's wife complained about her husband's allegiance to God. She even went so far as to tell him to curse God and die.

Tired of wandering in the wilderness for 40 years, the Israelites made no effort to hide their complaints from God. James 5:9 says, "...do not complain one against the other." Still, it goes on and on.

Today, we complain about the government, taxes, the high cost of automobile insurance, etc. Saint Frances DeSales says, "He who complains, sins." I'm sure, after all this time, God is tired of our complaining, faultfinding life-style. Frankly, the world (myself included) could use a lesson in unconditional surrender. As Christians we are supposed to, like that old church hymn *I surrender All* says, "surrender all." In doing so we take on the challenge of becoming more like Christ, loving, exhorting, encouraging, forgiving.

I object! To live a Christ-like life is too hard. Whoops, there I go again, down that same old complaining road again. Sorry.

The Accent Newspaper - 1996

All parts working together

In an issue of The Accent Newspaper, I misspelled the word, "Christianity." I had several phone calls asking, "What's christinity?" Christinity, folks is what happens when you leave the "a" out of the word Christianity.

In order to be effective in its meaning, the word "Christian" needs all its letters working together for the common good. Like faith. Without the "f" it's "aith", without the "a" "fith." It doesn't have the same meaning.

The body of Christ works the same way. It needs all the letters (parts), **P**resbyterian, **L**utheran, **C**atholic, **P**entecostal, **M**ethodist, working together for the good of the gospel. When one member is missing, or chooses not to participate in ministry, "Christianity" is not as effective as it could be.

I'm glad I'm a part of the family of God, where each and every member is equally important to God's kingdom.

Regarding the misspelled word, remember, to err is human, to forgive divine. Until next time, blessings, my friends.

Life is a Miracle

I once complained to God that I had never seen a miracle, and then I looked at my children! Everything they do in this life is a miracle! And if that isn't enough, I look at myself and think--I'm still here--now, that's a miracle!

Expect a miracle!

"Men talk about Bible miracles because there are no miracles in their lives." Henry David Thoreau

We put a new furnace in a few years ago. We have it all now, heat, air conditioning, and an air purifying machine. I was really excited about the air filtering device. I had convinced myself long before the installers came that it was going to make all the difference in the world in the air we would breathe. We are a family with allergies. Even though the installer told me not to expect results for at least 30 days, I knew, without doubt, we were going to breathe cleaner, fresher air in a matter of minutes.

"I can feel the difference in the air already," I told my husband an hour after the furnace man left.

"Don't be silly," he said, "it's too soon to notice a change."

Not to me. I had anticipated positive results and refused to accept anything less.

We should be the same way when it comes to prayer. We should look forward to it with anticipation, expecting positive results. Prayer works a lot like that air purifying machine. If you plug it in, and use it properly every day, you can expect good results. As Christians, we need to plug into our power source, God, daily. Pray as Thessalonias 5:17 instructs, without ceasing, then expect positive results--even a miracle!

I like what Matthew 21:22 has to say about prayer, "And all things you ask in prayer, believing you shall receive them."

Expecting a miracle is actually easier than we think.

The Accent - 1995

Communication gap

"Language is part of man's character." Francis Bacon

Henry Delacroix said, "An individual's whole life experience is built around his use of language." Which brings me to the great communication gap of the ages.

Today's words don't mean exactly what they used to. For example: "We had a gay time last night" could get you into a lot of trouble with some groups. A "dude" isn't necessarily a ranch hand and a "babe" is not a tiny little baby--if you get my drift. What does "get my drift" mean, anyway?

The last time I saw a roach it was an ugly bug. I wanted to call the exterminator immediately. Ask any teenager around and he'll give you a completely different definition of roach, angel dust and crack.

The world has gone bonkers when it comes to communication skills. It's nothing new. God had trouble communicating with his people. He was pretty adamant when he told Adam and Eve not to eat from the fruit of the tree of life in the middle of the garden, nor touch it, lest they would die. Yet, Eve did not heed those words of instruction, but instead, listened to the serpent and took the fruit and ate it and then gave it to Adam. And what about the doom of Sodom. If only the people would have listened to God and turned from their wicked ways, their lives would have been spared.

Genesis 10:5 says, "Nations were separated into their own lands, every one according to his language..." Corinthians 14:10 says, "There are, perhaps, many kinds of languages in the world, and not one kind is without meaning." So, what's the problem?

The answer is simple. Interpretation. Different meanings to different people. Another language barrier is lack of understanding. Sometimes, communication is simply misunderstood. The following story is a prefect example:

A woman went to court and told the judge she wanted a divorce.

"Do you have grounds?" The judge asked.

"Just two acres," she said.

"No, that's not it, lady. I mean, do you have a grudge?"

"No, we park the car in front of the house."

"Does your husband beat you up?" The frustrated judge wanted to know.

"No," she said. "I usually get up before he does."

"Then why exactly do you want a divorce? The judge asked.

"Because," the woman confessed, "we just don't seem to be able to communicate."

No matter what barriers may separate us, nothing can separate us from God and His universal language, love. It's a language the whole world understands.

The Accent - 1996

Garbage in--garbage out

"One must have an abundance of faith when God takes out the garbage." C. Hawkins

Have you ever noticed how the garbage piles up? It can sit there until it spills over onto the floor. No one takes it out. It doesn't seem to be anyone's job. Yet, someone has to take it upon themselves to remove the week's refuse, hopefully, before it starts to stink up the entire house.

I don't know about your house, but ours is full of garbage. Most of it gets rerouted to the garage or the basement. You know all the things you're saving, been saving for the past twenty years. All the junk you've been meaning to sort out and throw away, someday. Unfortunately, someday never seems to come--at least it hasn't come to our house, yet.

Every new year, I vow to make garbage my number one priority. I'm going to start with my office. My desk looks like a post office, mail waiting to be sorted, magazines piled up, letters from last year I still haven't answered. I have a neat filing system, everything goes in the top drawer of my computer stand. Hopefully, I'll get to the sorting-through process, later. How is it that we manage to collect so much stuff? Where does it all come from? Where does it go? If someone doesn't take control of the garbage situation soon, I fear our house is going to look like the city dump.

I think our spiritual life at times looks like a dump to God. Good thing He's a garbage collector! Every now and then, whether we like it or not, God sorts through the garbage in our life. The Bible calls it chastising. "Blessed is the man whom the Lord chastens..." Psalm 94:12. "For those whom the Lord loves He disciplines." Hebrews 12:6. I think God would love it if we'd just let go of the garbage in our lives, bury it, forget about it--work instead on cleansing body, soul, spirit and mind. What could be more important? If we did that, we wouldn't have to be chastised; there would be no garbage for God to sort through!

Today's special

"Soup and fish explain half of the emotions of life."
Sidney Smith

"If a man will be sensible and one fine morning, while he is laying in bed, count on the tips of his fingers how many things in this life truly give him enjoyment, invariably he will find food is the first one," says Chinaman Lin YuTang. "The Chinese," YuTang, went on to say "eat food for its textures, for the elastic, crisp effect it has on their teeth. They also eat and enjoy food," he said, "for its fragrance, flavor and color."

Americans on the other hand just enjoy eating. It doesn't really matter what they eat, apple dumplings, cheese, eggs, milk, hamburger or desserts. Everything we do in this society seems to revolve around food. Example, when was the last time somebody called and ask if you wanted to go bowling? It's always, "Let's go to lunch. I'll have my people call your people."

The Bible reminds us that our bodies are a temple unto the Lord and we should not put harmful things into it; that it is our Christian duty not to over indulge. Self-control is a fruit of the Spirit. Still, we continue to gorge, aware of, but unconcerned with the consequence obesity brings. I don't think Americans think of overeating and obesity as a sin. Even as Christians we fail to realize that man does not live by bread alone. We are forever breaking bread for one reason or another. America has more obesity and more fad diets than any other country in the world. And, we have Richard Simons sweating to the oldies to help us take it off!

The life-styles of today seem to be concentrating more and more on total wellness. Good nutrition, a balance diet (including vitamins, if you need them), is considered by man as preventative medicine. That coupled with exercise (keeping in shape), taking a breather from the demands of every day life (a vacation if you will), to reduce stress is all part of the "keeping fit and staying well" plan which, in the long run, equals a sound body, mind and spirit. In the summer months, the world especially thinks about "wellness." Americans everywhere are tying to shape up and slim down!

I go on a diet every January, every April and every June. I think I have tried every weight loss program known to man. I have lost the same 30 pounds three times--that's 90 pounds! Every year, I vow no more procrastination on losing weight. I have been a member of TOPS, Weight Watchers, Jenny Craig and even joined the diet support group at my church when they offered a free weight-loss seminar--no fees, no gimmicks--no foolin'! The instructors who taught the seminar had lost, between the two of them, a total of 300 pounds! They looked in the peak of health. *Hey, I can do this* I thought to myself.

It suddenly occurred to me--the Bible has a plan of attack for everything. There must be a spiritual approach to dieting. If God loves and cares for us, He obviously cares about our weight as well. In turning to the scriptures I found tons (pardon the pun) of verses relating to the well being of our bodies. "Man does not live by bread alone." Deuteronomy 8:3. "Present your bodies a living sacrifice..." Romans 12:1. "You are a temple of God, the Spirit of God dwells in you." I Corinthians 3:26. The list goes on and on, but the reality is, God gave us one body. It is our job to keep it strong and healthy. We can't do that if we are constantly putting harmful things into it. Cake, cookies, and potato chips are just as harmful as drugs and alcohol.

Dieting in itself doesn't seem to be the answer. In fact, a report in *Wellness Today*, May '92, revealed that diets can slow down your metabolism and actually cause your body to store more fat. "Dieting," the article said, "can also lead to a dangerous cycle of depriving yourself until your willpower gives out, and you give in."

Once that happens we have an excuse to "pig out." What and where is the answer?

According to the *Wellness Today* report, part of the answer comes in developing a good food plan, one that allows you to eat several small meals a day. The idea behind this theory is that your stomach will stay full and you won't feel hungry or be tempted to blow it. As I was reading that article I found myself thinking--*this will never work.*

Biblically, God has temptation covered, too. The Bible says in II Peter that, "The Lord knows how to rescue the godly from temptation." God supports our weakness. Hebrews 4:16 tells us to "draw near with confidence to the throne of grace...that we may find the grace needed to help us in our time of need..." God is faithful, He will not allow us to be tempted beyond our ability to handle it. Let's not forget that verse we learned as children in Sunday school, "...lead us not into temptation..." Matthew 6:13.

Perhaps, the real answer to successful dieting lies in learning to exercise self-control. If we can learn that simple lesson, the rest will be easy. But don't take my word for it, put God to the test and try His plan for yourself. According to His plan we can lose weight and keep it off! After all, is not life more than food? In the meantime, praise the Lord and pass the celery!

Bay City Times - 1992

Recipes to help you lose weight

Once again I turn to my special second grade friends to help me with recipes to keep me fit and trim. I'm sure, if you give them a try, they will do the same for you. (Recipes are unedited).

Cooked rice & a sandwich:
First, put 1/2 cup of water in a small pan. Cook the water until it is boiling, then, put in 1/2 of rice. Cook it for a couple of minutes until it boils again. Dump it into a 1/2 cup dish. Then put a bun in the microwave to unfreeze it. Cook some rolled around chicken for 1/2 hour. Poke some toothpicks in it to see if it is done. If it isn't, flip it over on the other side for 5 minutes. Put it on the bun with a scooper so you don't burn your fingers. Knife on some mayonnaise and two piece of lettuce.

Toocos:
First buy eight tooco shells, a pound of hamburger, a package of sliced cheese and a head of salad. Cook the hamburger in a fry pan for about a half hour. Cut up the salad with a knife and put it on a plate. Put the cheese on another plate. Warm the shell in a different fry pan for as long as the hamburger. When they are ready, bend the shells and scoop up some hamburger with a spatula. Then goes the cheese and salad. If the shell gets holes in the bottom, the hamburger will fall on your plate. Be sure to use a fork to pick it up so you're not messy.

Rice cakes:
Get a large rice cake, put on drops of peanut butter. This is very good for a diet 'cept the rice cakes are very dry. That's why they are good for diets--nobody likes them!

Baked turkey:

Buy a turkey that weights a whole pound. Put it in a big square pan. Dump in about a quarter of water so it keeps cool and won't burn. By some regular turkey stuffing in a box. Take it out of the package and heat it in a round pan for 1/2 hour. Take it out and cool it some. Then hold the turkey with some corn snipers and shovel the stuffing in with a spoon. Put it in so it won't fall out. Put the whole thing in the oven and warm it for 55 minutes. The oven should be 250 on the dial. Then take it out and let it cool so it won't burn your mouth when you eat it!

Fruit salad:

Get out a large bowel. Peel 10 oranges and two apples. Take out the seeds with the edge of a knife. Turn on the water in the sink and wash 10 grapes. Dry them with a towel and set them in with the oranges and apples. Spoon on a half of a butter tub of whipped cream. Stir it by rubbing on the sides so you don't hurt the fruit. Set it in the refrigerator so it gets cold, about a half an hour.

Salad:

Start with a leaf of salad, add a mountain of cottage on top and a side slice of peach in juice. Then give yourself one piece of pickle, the sour kind. No milk, drink water instead.

Our son Matthew's recipe for basghetti:

Get a middle pan. Put in a box (1/2 box) of basghetti and a little water. Cook it for 1/2 hour. Get out the water with a 'holy' pan. Fry up a package of hamburger for a few minutes and drop in 15 hole mushrooms and two onions all cut up. (I don't like the onions). Cook for 2 1/2 hours. When it bubbles you can stop cooking and start eating!

Let's not forget my favorite--desserts!

Cake:

Put a chocolate chip cake mix into a great big yellow bowel. Put two teaspoons of water and two or three eggs that are cracked. I get to mix it with the electric beaters for 8 minutes. Spoon it into a rectangle pan and put it in a oven on medium hot for 10 or 11 minutes. Then the buzzer rings. Cool it first before you put the frosting on or it will melt.

Frosting: Get a bag of frosting powder and put it in with whatever is left from the cocoa can. Pour in an inch of water. Mix it with the beaters, spoon it on the cake in a big glob and knife it around. Now it's done. Save the beaters and knife and spoon for your kids to lick.

Jello:

Put the red stuff from a jello box into scalding water, put in frig. When it gets solid, eat it with a plastic spoon. PS: Don't wait 'til it gets rubbery--it won't taste good then.

Recipes compiled by the Second Grade Class
Linwood Elementary School where our son was
a student.
Copyright 1986 - All rights reserved

Writing is unedited and presented just as it
was given to me. Thanks to all those who
contributed their recipes.

Matthew's Food Barn
(This section of writing is unedited)

If you're like me and you hate cooking, or you simply don't feel like cooking, you could eat out at Matthew's Food Barn. He says he has the best prices in town, guaranteed. And, says Chef Matthew, "You can get a glass of water with any order!"

Here's a sample of what the Food Barn has to offer:

Cod Fish & Water, perch Fish or Cat Fish - $5.95
Turkey with brocklay or baked chicken for lunch - $5.00
Oat bran panacakes for only $5.50 (for those who prefer breakfast instead of lunch).
One egg/no yolk - $3.99 (for those cholesterol watchers).
Breakfast bar (if you're really hungry) - $6.99
*Free cup of orange juice with any breakfast order, compliments of Chef Matt.

Matthew wants you to know he has standard hamburgers with fries and cheeseburgers with fries or a minnie tocoo, all ready and waiting hot on the grill! You can also get a whopper, chicken sandwich or Big Mac without going to those perspective eateries.

If you don't want hamburgers or tocoos, you can always order two hole pizzas with 2 toppings for only $20, or just two pieces of pizza or even a pocket pizza. (Is that a pizza you can put in your pocket and take home to eat later?)

For all you crazy dieters, there is also a salad bar at the Food Barn, regular or chefs. (We might even offer tocoo salads--if you ask for it.)

Something new at the Food Barn this year is curly chips for 50 cents a bag. Now, that's a bargain. What are curly chips you ask? They're chips that are curled on the end. (Like curly fries--only chips).

45

Also available to the diet conscious crowd is chicken noodle soup without the noodles to save on calories, and cabbage soup made with plenty of cabbage, which help you poop!

And there's plenty of ice cream for those hot summer days. Flavors are: strawberry, venelia, chalket, supper man, reshberry, mackinaw fuge, twist, cheery and very blue berry.

Monday at the Barn is sale day--50 cents off on all food. Tuesday is 25 cents more. Matthew suggest you visit the Food Barn on Monday because Monday is a slow day.

The Grand Buffet is every day all day long for $5--all you can get--limit is one plate of food per person, please.

On your way out, go to the front desk to pay the check!

HAVE A GOOD DAY~

(*Matthew was 7 or 8 when he wrote this*)

It's a riot to diet

Give me little white onions cooked in creamed peas
Perfectly cut asparagus spears, if you please
Pickled beets and artichoke hearts
All piled up in my shopping cart.

Tatter tots and tocos hot--chicken lean and French cuisine
Cottage cheese and Goober Peas
And lean, mean pork chops sliced very thin
All in the cart--toss 'em in.

On the way to the checkout line--
One last stop
Gotta pick up some diet pop
Isn't life a riot when you're on a diet!

46

Stories from behind the pulpit

"Story telling is not art, but we call it a knack."
Sir Richard Steele

Working as a freelance writer for eight years and later as the editor of my own Christian centered newspaper, I've heard plenty of stories told from behind the pulpit. Here are a few of my favorites. I hope you will enjoy them as much as I have.

Nobody's Home

"Hello, Son. I'm Rev. Wilson from the Wesleyan Church, is your father at home?"
"I think so."
"Do you think I could speak to him?"
"I don't see why not."
"When can I see him?"
"Right now, I guess."
"Could you go tell your father I'm here."
"Ok."
Several minutes later the young lad returns.
"Did you tell your father I want to see him?"
"Yes I did."
"And does he want to see me?"
"Yes he does."
"Should I wait here for him?"
"If you want to."
"Several more minutes pass.
"I thought you said your father was home?"
"He is," said the boy, "but I don't live here. I live across the street!"

This story was told to me by a Lutheran pastor's wife.

Yes, we have no celery today

Our daughter was seen all over town, going door-to-door, collecting vegetables in her little red wagon.

"Why are you collecting vegetables? Is your mother making stew?" One of the parishioners, a board member asked.

"Oh, no," the little girl replied. "No stew. I'm collecting vegetables because Mommy is tired of being poor as a church mouse. Do you got any celery?"

"No, but I have some carrots you can have."

"Thank you, but I'd rather have celery. My dad said if he had a decent celery we wouldn't have to live like pallbearers."

"I think you mean paupers, Dear. I'll see what I can do about getting your family a decent celery."

"Thank you very much."

Mother learns of birth first

I was a sophomore in high school when I taught my first Sunday school class. It was December. We were studying the birth of the baby Jesus.

"Who do you think was the first to learn of the baby's birth?" I asked, thinking the wisemen or the shepherds would be a suitable answer.

The pastor's daughter raised a small, timid hand. "His mother, I hope," she proudly answered.

By Connie Hawkins

Let's talk about nothing

If you think kids aren't paying attention in church, think again. A young, student teacher in a Lutheran school, shared this story with me about his first teaching experience--a group of fifth grade students --tough audience.

Realizing that stories and puppets wouldn't work with the 10 and 11 year old age group, he asked them what they wanted to talk about.

"Nothing," one young man proclaimed.

"We can't spend the next several weeks talking about nothing," the teacher explained. "It would get pretty boring."

"Why not," said the boy. "My dad says the pastor goes on for months and says nothing!"

Thou shalt not interrupt thy prayers

A Catholic priest told this tale.

There was a woman in my parish who faithfully attended Mass every single day. In 20 years she had not missed one single morning of prayer.

One morning two young altar boys saw that she had paused to kneel in front of the blessed Virgin Mary to pray, and decided to play a prank on the elderly woman.

"This is Jesus," they whispered from the balcony, "do you need anything special today, dear saint?"

The woman kept up her prayer vigil without so much as a blink of an eye.

"Hail down there, it's Jesus up here," the boys spoke a little louder.

Paying little attention, the woman continued to pray.

"I say," the boys shouted, "it's the Son."

Finally the woman looked up. "I'll be with you in a moment. I'm speaking to your mother right now," she returned their banter without missing a single bead on her rosary!

49

Taking a vacation is for the birds

I love this story told by an Episcopal priest.

Father Brown decided to take a vacation, the first in several years. He didn't want to leave the parsonage unattended while he and his wife were away so he bought a parrot and a dog to keep watch over the place.

"Now, Mary, you're in charge of the house while I'm gone," he instructed the parrot, "so take good care of things."

"Take care," the bird squawked, "take care."

The Browns weren't gone two days when a thief entered the dwelling. He headed for the kitchen.

"Don't touch that silver," Mary squawked.

"And why not?" The thief asked.

"Number eight," the bird bellowed. "Thou shalt not steal."

The thief laughed, "Who are you? The Mother Mary?"

"I'm Mary," the bird squealed.

"Cute." The thief shrugged off Mary's warning and proceeded about his business--to collect the silver.

"Put that silver down!" the bird ordered, "or Jesus will get you!"

"Jesus will get me," the thief mocked.

"Don't touch those candlesticks! Jesus will get you," Mary's high-pitched screech was starting to get on the thief's nerves.

Silence. Had the thief left? "Thief, are you there?" Mary called out.

"I'm here, bird."

"Don't you want the gold cuff links in the bedroom?" the parrot stammered.

"Good idea. Thanks, bird."

"Just remember, I warned you--Jesus will get you."

"Right." The thief laughed as he threw open the door to the master bedroom, only to face the largest Doberman he had ever seen.

"Get 'em, Jesus!" the bird ordered.

Walking on water

A Presbyterian minister shared this story.

A priest, a minister and a rabbi were out fishing in a small rowboat.

"I'm thirsty," said the rabbi. "I think I'll go ashore for a cold drink."

"Great idea," said the priest. "Bring us all back a drink."

The rabbi got out of the boat, walked on water and returned a few minutes later with a jug of cold tea.

"That really hit the spot," the priest said, "but now I'm hungry. I think I'll go ashore for some sandwiches."

"Good idea," said his fellow clergy.

The priest got out of the boat, walked on water and returned several minutes later with sandwiches.

"You know," said the minister, "I could go for some dessert."

Us, too," agreed the rabbi and the priest.

The minister got out of the boat and fell into the water. He was dismayed. How was it that his fellow clergymen were able to walk on water while he sank? Perhaps, he did not have enough faith in the Master to keep him afloat. He tried again, and again he sank.

The priest and the rabbi looked over the edge of the boat at their flailing friend.

"Do you think," said the rabbi," we should tell Rev. Jones about the stepping stones?"

Calling all MPs

Most of us have probably heard about the WC, (the water commode) and the Wesleyan Church, but have you head the one about the MP, the Methodist pastor?

A woman moving to Milwaukee was planning on joining the Methodist Church when she got there. She had heard rumors about what an effective leader the Methodist pastor was and wanted to find out more about him and his church. She decided to contact the Chamber of Commerce about the number of churches in the area and to find out what she could about the Methodist pastor. To make a long story short, she simply referred to the Methodist pastor as the MP.

The Chamber thinking the woman must surely mean the Milwaukee Police sent her the following reply:

I think you will find the MP to your liking. You asked about membership. Because of rapid growth, we have had to build a larger facility just to house the MP. Does the MP do good work? We think so. My wife, and several other women in the community, worked diligently with the MP last month and were very impressed with the MP's ability to get jobs done.

The MP does an outstanding job in the community. Last June, the women of the MP, of which my wife is one, were honored by the Civic Club for their charitable contributions to human services and other organizations--with more contributions promised. The MP is very busy.

You asked about public speaking. The MP does a fine job and is always available at a moment's notice to speak to both profit and nonprofit functions. Last month the MP was in jail and the month before that in the hospital! The MP has spoken at several organizations about "shady" projects like planting trees in our downtown parks. The MP also finds time to case homes on behalf of the homeless and those involved in crime.

The MP is especially fond of babies and small children. The women of the MP are ecstatic that the MP is so family-oriented. There are at least 27 children in the organization, and more on the way!

As far as salary goes, I am proud to say our MP is the highest paid in he state and we intend to keep it that way.

Thank you for your interest in the MP. We look forward to meeting you upon your arrival here and hope that your stay with us will be a long and prosperous one. We know, if you are working with the MP, your time with us will be well spent.

Parable of a dead church

The following came to me via a local church newsletter. Paraphrasing, I am happy to share the story with you.

A man called a local pastor one day. He wanted to join the church, but went on to explain that he didn't want to worship every week, study the Bible or visit the sick, serve as a leader, or witness to a non-Christian. The pastor commended him for his desire to join the congregation, but told him the church he sought was located in another section of town. The man took down the directions, hung up and went off to locate the church.

Amazingly, when the man arrived at the church, he came face to face with the logical result of his own apathetic attitude. There stood an abandoned church building boarded up and ready for demolition.

The church cannot afford apathetic Christians--there's already too many abandoned churches across America. Let's gear up for what lies ahead by showing willingness to attend Sunday morning worship, study the Bible, visit the sick and shut-in, witness to our fellowman, serving God by serving the local church.

The Accent Newspaper - June 1966

53

I cannot end this section of the book without one of my all time favorite stories. A similar story appeared in Ann Landers column some years ago, and again recently. I like to refer to this version as the Christian account of *Don't mess with Sex.*

"Hi, Son, I'm Rev. Davis. I'm here to see your deacon father. Will you kindly tell him I've arrived for our appointment."

"Ok."

"What took you so long?"

"I was out looking for Sex."

"Really...do your parents know that you are looking for sex?"

"It was their idea."

"I see. Well, as a man of the cloth, I don't think you should be looking for sex."

"Why not?"

"You're much too young."

"How old do you have to be to look for Sex?"

"I'm not sure, but I do know you should be married, first."

"Why?"

"Because the Bible says so, that's why. The good book says it's a sin to look for sex before marriage."

"I didn't know that."

"Well, now you do."

"Does that mean my sister can't look for Sex, either?"

"I don't know, is she married?"

"No, she's even younger than me."

"Then, she shouldn't look for sex, either."

"No looking for Sex until you're married, right?"

"That's right, Son."

"This is going to break my sister's heart. If we don't find Sex now, we probably won't find Sex for a long time. Maybe we'll never find Sex."

"Why are you looking so sad?"

"Because we've had Sex for a long time. It's going to be hard on us not having Sex anymore."

"You mean, you and your sister have sex?"

"Ya, together. It's really going to be tough with no Sex in our house."

"I understand," said the pastor. "But trust me, this is all for the best."

"I don't suppose you've seen Sex?"

"Not lately," the pastor admitted.

"Have you ever seen Sex?"

"Occasionally." The pastor's face turned beet red.

"When was the last time you saw Sex, Pastor?"

"I hardly think that's any of your business young man." The pastor loosened the knot on his tie. "When was the last time you seen, Sex, boy?"

"This morning in the kitchen."

"In the kitchen!" The pastor was appalled. "And where else have you seen sex?"

"In the bathroom, sometimes in my sister's room. We usually fight over whose room we should have Sex in. Mom says Sex is dirty and should be in the garage. I don't like Sex in the garage--it's cold out there."

"I take it your mother doesn't care for sex?"

"She hates Sex. She never liked Sex. She says Sex gives her a headache. Grandma doesn't like Sex, either. But Grandpa loves Sex. He says Sex is good for old people."

"Young man, I've had just about enough of all this sex talk. I demand to speak to your father and mother immediately."

"Ok, but Dad can't talk right now."

"Why not?"

"He's out with our neighbor looking for Sex."

"And your mother?"

"She's upstairs crying about Sex right now."

"Son, Mrs. Robinson and I found Sex in Mrs. Herman's garage--isn't that great? Oh, Rev. Davis, I wasn't expecting you until after supper."

"Obviously."

"I'm sorry I wasn't here. I was out looking..."

"I know," interrupted the pastor. "You were out looking for sex. Do you know what YOUR son has been up to while you were out?"

"Looking for Sex, I hope. We should all be looking for Sex."

"How disgusting. I'm afraid you'll have to resign from the Board of Deacons, immediately. What is that beguiling looking creature?"

"That's our German shepherd, Sexton. We call him Sex for short. Mom, you'd better bring Rev. Davis a glass of water. Sex made him faint.

"Wh-o are you?" Rev. Davis, barely recovered from his ordeal with Sex, asked a blond-haired little girl peering over him.

"I'm Sara, I live across the street. Who are you?"

"I'm Rev. Davis."

"Nice to meet you, Sir. Have you seen my Sox?"

"Your socks? What color?"

"Yellow. I can't believe I lost my Sox, again."

"I'm sure you'll find your socks. When did you last see your socks?"

"In the pantry, I think. Mother told me to put Sox in the basement for a good washing. I didn't do it and now I've lost my Sox."

"What do you usually do with socks after a good washing?"

"I usually put Sox in my room so Sox will stay clean."

"Doesn't everybody?" Rev. Davis asked.

"Not my friend, Nancy. She keeps hers in the kitchen in a box."

"Socks in a box in the kitchen, how interesting."

"Her's are black and white. Her mother says she has way to many, that she should give some away."

"I don't think she can part with them though. I bet Sox ran after Sex."

"Is Sox a dog by any chance?"

"No, silly. Sox is my cat."

"I suppose Sox likes Sex?"

"Sure, doesn't everybody?"

"I have to go home now. I feel another headache coming on."

"Too much talk about Sex, huh? I understand. Good day, Rev. Davis. I hope you feel better soon. Come back and play with my Sox, anytime!"

First comes marriage--then a baby carriage

"It's not lack of love, but lack of friendship
that makes unhappy marriages." Friedrich Nietzsche

*Bill and Connie sittin' in a tree K-I-S-S-I-N-G. First comes
love, then comes marriage. Then comes Connie pushing a baby
carriage.* I hated that jump rope chant! I still do.

In the beginning marriage was good. Bill and I continued to
live in the apartment I was renting before I met him, a small place in
a rundown neighborhood close to the GM plant where he worked as
a millwright. I couldn't afford anything grander. At least when Bill
moved in, the place got a fresh coat of paint and I got a new bed! The
old one, if you could call it a bed, with it's creaky springs and sagging
mattress, had seen better days.

We both worked. I had a job as a medical insurance biller in
a doctor's office. There was plenty of money, enough to buy anything
we needed. Evenings were spent riding around on Bill's motorcycle,
cruising the car lots for the new car we expected to buy, hopefully a
sporty little number. I could easily picture us riding, or sailing as it
were, off into the sunset in some pricey sports car.

But it was not to be. Six months after we were married we
bought a ranch-style house in the suburbs, settling for a midsize
family-to-be kind of car. Tranquility gave way in our home when
Heidi and Matthew came long and we bought a station wagon!

A Thursday's child with far to go, Heidi came into the world
May 1, 1975. She weighed almost 10 pounds when she was born.
We had to take back all those cute new born outfits. Her wrinkled
brow and pouty little smile, which earned her the nickname "baby
pouty", could melt your heart. She was a daddy's girl right from the
start, which boggles my mind because now that she's grown, she and
her dad can't seem to get along no matter what they do. Anyway, she
and I never bonded well. In the hospital whenever I would try to feed

her she would wail nonstop until a frazzled nurse arrived to see what all the fuss was about. However, the minute her father stepped into the room she'd coo like a morning dove. I had a terrible case of postpartum blues that lasted 23 years!

The day the doctor discharged me I called my mother to come and get me. I couldn't wait until 3:00 when Bill's shift let out. All I wanted to do was to get out of that hospital and into my own house. Mom diligently helped me pack up the gifts and flowers I had received while in the hospital. One good thing about being in the hospital is gifts and fruit. Why do visitors bring fruit, anyway? Oh, now I remember, constipation--the memory is coming back to me. If you don't have it when you go into the hospital--you'll have it when you leave! Fresh fruit is supposed to be good for that.

While Mom helped me get ready to leave, an OB nurse dressed Heidi, carefully explaining home care procedures and how important getting the baby settled into a routine would be.

Routine. What did I care about routine. If she continued to wail at every feeding I would be giving her away before we even left the parking lot! The nurse stuck me in a wheelchair, lap loaded with a suitcase full of goodies, potted plants and little frilly dresses, of which Heidi never wore; she never was the "frilly" type. I threw out most of the plants. The ones I did keep died.

"Aren't you forgetting something?" The nurse asked as Mom was about to wheel me out of the room.

"I don't think so," I said.

She pointed to the small bundle in her arms.

"Oh, the girl. Would you mind," I smiled. "I'm pretty loaded down here."

From that moment on, Heidi became known as "the girl." When her brother arrived three years later, he was dubbed, "the boy." They didn't know they had names until they started school! Whenever we went anywhere I got "the boy" ready and Bill took care of "the girl."

Once settled in the car, I urged Mom to hurry and start the engine.

"Are you sure you've got everything? I feel as if we are forgetting something," she fretted.

"Nonsense," I said. "Let's go. Start the car."

A light tapping on the window interrupted that process. The nurse stood outside the car still holding a now squirming baby in her arms. And why shouldn't the little tyke squirm. It was an 80 degree May day and I had her dressed in a blue knitted sweater! We were expecting a boy. Everything was blue! Besides, Bill's grandmother knitted the outfit special for home coming. I was not known for veering from a set plan.

"I knew we were forgetting something!" Mother was horrified. How could I forget my own baby?

"Do we have to take her home?" I pouted. "She hates me."

"Nonsense," Mom said. "She's just a little baby. She doesn't even know what hate is. You'll adjust."

I never did adjust.

Heidi graduated from college and is working as a social worker down state. Hopefully, if she's developed a complex from my reaction to motherhood--she got counseling! As for me, nothing's changed. I'm still trying to adjust.

Thursday's child

"A woman never loafs; she shops, entertains
and visits." E. H. Howe

Heidi backed into the kitchen from the garage, arms loaded
with suitcases, laundry bag, and a box full of junk she thinks's she
going to store in the basement.

"Something smells good," she kicks the door shut with her
foot. "Is it stir fry?"

"It's goulash," I answer.

"Goulash. You know I hate goulash!"

"You hate everything I cook."

She was always a picky eater. When she was a baby she had
colic and couldn't keep her formula down. I can still remember
walking the floor nights--tearing my hair out days. When she was
three all she would eat was hot dogs. That changed to macaroni and
cheese when she was ten. In junior high it was cereal. She lived on
Fruit Loops all through high school. Now, she hates hot dogs, can't
stand the smell of macaroni and refuses to eat cereal. It doesn't matter
what I cook, she doesn't like it!

"Doesn't this goulash look good?" I lifted the lid on the pot.

She wrinkled her nose. "It's gross. I hate tomatoes. And you
know I don't like hamburger meat. Why can't you make goulash
without tomatoes and hamburger in it?"

"Then it wouldn't be goulash, it would be noodles," I explain.

"So, what else is there to eat?"

"I made a cake."

"Is it lemon?"

"It's carrot. I know you hate carrots, but it's all I had in the
cupboard."

"You didn't put real carrot peelings in it, did you? You always try to do that and it never works."

"Carrots are good for you," I justify. "They're good for your eyes. Have you ever seen a rabbit wearing glasses?" I asked.

Rolling her beautiful blue eyes, she plops her paraphernalia in the middle of the living room. *Why can't she walk the extra few feet to her room and dump her stuff there?* I wonder to myself.

"I have to do my laundry," she announces as if reading my thoughts.

"Of course you do. Don't they have laundromats in that college town of yours?"

"I can't afford to do laundry in one of those dreadful places. Besides those laundry mat people rip you off. Not to mention those buildings smell! And you don't know who used the machine before you, of if they cleaned it!"

"Did you at least bring your own soap?"

"Dah," she produces detergent and softner.

What kind of word is "dah" anyway?

"Can't you eat a little bite of goulash," I say over supper. "You're nothing but skin and bones."

"Are you on the subject of my thinness again?" She pouts. "Give my portion to Mattie, he'll eat anything."

"You're so stubborn," I argue.

"It wouldn't hurt you to eat some goulash," her father injects.

"Why should I eat something I don't like?"

"To please your mother; it'll make her happy."

"Like she ate to please Grandma?"

"My mother is an excellent cook, "I remind everyone.

"Obviously, look at you now. You have love handles. Soon you'll have to shop at Arnolds Tent and Awning Company."

"That's not a nice thing to say," her father chides. "Besides, Arnolds went out of business last month."

"Very funny," I say. "You should talk, Dear. Your stomach

looks like a big, round basketball." I poke my husband in places that he preferred I not touch. The food war was on. We spend the next several minutes arguing over who has the most weight to lose and what kind of foods we should eat to achieve those results.

"Hey, Sis, when did you get home?" Matthew comes in late for supper as usual. Considering this kid owns three watches, and collects clocks, you'd think he could be on time for meals!

"I got in last night." Heidi answers his question. "If you wouldn't spend so much time at your girlfriend's house, you'd remember that you have a sister."

"Now I remember why I don't miss you when you're at school"

"How come you never write to me?" Heidi demands of her brother. "I've been in college for three years now and what do I get; three letters from home and that's if I'm lucky!"

"I don't know how to write, remember? Besides, you're only an hour away. It's faster to drive and easier to call."

"A call? You mean like on the telephone?" The banter never stops.

"What's for supper?" Matthew falls into his chair. He never sits, he falls. Most men fall into their chairs. Why is that? Why can't they just simply lower their bodies down onto the seat like normal people? No, they have to plunk, slough, slide, glide or fall.

"Is that goulash I smell? If Heidi was coming home, Mom, why'd you make goulash. You know she hates goulash." He answers his own question. "I, on the other hand, love it. It's one of my favorites." He fills his plate.

"Everything Mom makes is your favorite," his sister reminds him. "And you know Mom hates me," Heidi affirms. "That's why she made goulash."

"I don't hate you," I said. "I thought you hated me."

"Why would I hate my own mother. That's absurd. "And even if I did hate you, once. That's over now. I'm a social science major for gosh sakes. I can cope with love/hate relationships."

63

"Then it's true. You do hate me?"

"I didn't say that." She rolls consuming eyes as she heads towards the cupboard. "I don't know where you get these ideas."

"They're implied," I said as I put a piece of carrot cake on her plate. "Here, try this."

She shoves the plate aside. "I don't like carrot cake," she stubbornly reminds me. "You know I only like lemon flavored cake."

"If the truth were know, you hate food period. Just like you hate your mother," Matthew chided. "Give the cake to Dad, Mom. He'll eat any kind of cake."

"I don't like chocolate," he reminds everyone. With his birthday just around the corner, I'm positive he wants to make sure he isn't getting chocolate treats of any kind. It was good to hear his voice. I wasn't sure he was paying attention. It's hard to tell if he's listening around the dinner table. He usually says little during meals, or anytime else for that matter.

Everyone in the house pretty much knows Bill's routine. He comes home from work, heads for the john with the paper, is the first one done eating, heads for the TV, snoozes in his lazy boy and then goes to bed. I won't allow the television on while we're eating. It's annoying, besides, meal times in our family has always been a bonding time. It's a rule. The only problem is no one ever bonds. All we do is argue, but at least we're communicating!

"When are you coming home, again?" I ask both kids.

"Why?"

"Family reunion time."

"You know I hate reunions," Matt winches.

"I don't even know half those people," Heidi whines.

"That's the purpose of a reunion to get to know your relatives."

"Right." The eye-rolling, again. "What's the point?"

"It's good to check in," I defend. "You find out who's married to who, who's getting a divorce, who's not talking to whom. You get to know your cousins."

"Which ones?"

"The ones you don't know, obviously."

"Do I really want to know them?" Heidi asks.

"Probably not," Matt says.

Now it's my turn for some eye-rolling.

"Why are you even going, Mom? You don't even like half your relatives," Matt wants to know.

"Well, I can fraternize with the half I do like. Besides, my brother owes me $3 for his half of our long distance phone bill. And I owe him $5 for somebody's funeral flowers."

"Somebody in the family died? Who? Why didn't anybody tell me? I'm always the last to know these things," Heidi pouts.

"I didn't think you cared."

"Well, it depends on who it was...is it anybody I know?"

"You don't know anybody because you won't go to family reunions!" I'm quick to point out. "It was Uncle Henry, if you must know," I politely relate.

"Uncle Henry, who's he?"

"My point exactly. Need I say more."

"Dad, did you know Uncle Henry died?"

Henry? Henry who? You don't have a Henry in your family."

"I do so. My mother's stepfather was Henry."

"And he just died?" Bill's shocked. "How come nobody told me?"

"Wow!" Heidi proclaims, "the old guy must have been a hundred and something."

"I thought Henry's name was Hank."

"They're both the same name, Matt." Heidi tells her brother and she should know, after all, she's in college she knows everything.

"Hank. Henry--it doesn't matter. He died when I was young."

"And you're just burying him, now. Unbelievable," Matt whistles.

"Forget it," tossing my cloth napkin in the trash (I forgot it wasn't paper) I start clearing the table. "It's time to do dishes."

"I have to finish my laundry," Heidi heads for the basement.

"My car's making a funny noise," Matthew heads to the garage.

"What about you?" My eyes follow Bill into the living room where he "plunks" down into his recliner.

"I worked all day, I'm tired," he says.

"Like I do nothing but sit around the house day in and day out."

"Well," he grunts, if the shoe fits, wear it. Managing a newspaper isn't work, neither is writing a book. Everybody knows that. All you do is sit at the computer all day. How much work can that be?"

Why is it just because you work at home, nobody thinks you work?

"Faith is the soul riding anchor. Josh Billings said that."

"Who in the heck is Josh Billings, and what's it supposed to mean?" Bill looks confused.

"Never mind, you wouldn't get it."

"Obviously," he says. "I'm not sure you get it."

Families. I need a vacation from mine!

"Perhaps the greatest social service that can be rendered by anybody to the country and to mankind is to bring up a family; but here again, because there is nothing to sell, there is a very general disposition to regard a married woman's work as no work at all, and to take it as a matter of course that she should be paid for it."
George Bernard Shaw

Cousins

"Every family has a prized kin." E.W. Howe

When we go to Grandma's house
Things sure are a buzzin'
We've got so many aunts and uncles
We've got cousins by the dozens

We've got cousins in the hallway
And cousins in the chair
And if you look behind the door--
You'll find a cousin there

We've got a cousin in the bath tub
Two cousins under Grandpa's bed
And a cousin in the playroom
Standing on her head

We've got cousins in the kitchen
And a cousin where Grandma keeps her broom
We've got so many cousins--
There isn't any room

We've got cousins that are big and tall
And cousins that are very small
We've got baby cousins, too
Cousin girls and cousin boys

Oh, oh, oh--the noise!

Monday's child

"No self-made man ever did such a good job that
some woman didn't want to make a few alterations."
Kin Hubbard

Fair of face is Monday's child. Matthew, born on July 3, 1978, was almost a Yankee doodle dandy baby. He missed it by a few hours; something about the doctor--Fourth of July--and golf!

Matthew's biggest complaint about being born the day before a holiday is that no one is ever around to celebrate his birthday. They're all up north celebrating Uncle Sam's birthday. For years we had his cake on the last Saturday in June. It wasn't until he reached his teens that he realized his birthday wasn't June 30th, but July 3rd!

From day one, Matthew was a home body, a real mama's boy. A very private person, he resented the intrusion strangers--or anybody for that matter--brought into his home. I remember the time the insurance man dropped by to discuss upgrading Bill's policy. Evidently, he stayed an hour longer than Matthew deemed necessary. Barely three at the time, "the boy" dragged the man's heavy trench coat from the couch, handed him his hat and pointed to the door. Apparently, it was time to go. It wasn't just strangers that Matthew showed a cold shoulder. There were times he wouldn't give his own grandmother the time of day. He would turn his face away when she would try to kiss him on the cheek, but he always took the lifesaver she offered as a token of peace. Now that he's grown, nothing has changed. He still prefers staying home to going out and he still doesn't like strangers invading his personal space. Company is ok, if he knows they are coming and he's ready for them. He still likes lifesavers only now he prefers breath mints!

Heidi pretty much did what she was told and didn't have any trouble entertaining herself when she was small. You could always trust her to play quietly in her room. Matthew on the other hand was

68

"Mr. Mischief." He liked to take things apart--still does. If the toy industry stated on their labels that something was "absolutely" child-proof, Matthew would prove them wrong by disassembling the product. Heidi is still angry because he took her doll buggy apart and couldn't remember how to put it back together! He did the same thing to his Fisher Price record player. Come to think of it, he did the same thing to my stereo! I'm still finding parts scattered all over the garage! But trying to reconstruct the cuckoo clock my brother sent me from German was going a bit too far. The clock is up in the attic somewhere, still broken. I'm going to give it to Matthew when he gets married for a wedding present. Hopefully, by then, he'll be able to fix it!

Matthew is all boy. As a child, he liked to skip rope, climb trees, dig in the garden, and slide down the ditch on a saucer in the winter. He was riding a two-wheel bike by the age of five and couldn't wait to get a car! He had a pet toad until I told him he'd get a wart on his nose if he brought it into the house, again. No more toads; the next critter he brought home was a snake. I think it's still living in our garage!

Matthew was, and still is, a great collector of things. Match box cars, legos, transformers and other little plastic toys that drives a mother nuts, especially when you step on them! As he grew older his collection changed to yo-yos, key chains to the many cars he's owned, and sports posters.

While other boys spent hours digging in the dirt, tossing the football around or perfecting their baseball skills, Matthew was banging on pots and pans, a born drummer. Instead of stacking blocks, he chose to stack cans of food--the artist in him! A chip off of my block, he's an artist and a musician, playing both piano and guitar, and he won the "Young Author's Award" twice!

Like most boys, we can't seem to fill him up. He eats anything and everything, even Brussel sprouts! He never refuses to try something new, well maybe, liver. One of his goals at age 10, was to win a gold medal for eating the most pizza. He's a lean, mean eating machine! Nothing's changed. He still likes to eat, but so do I. And I have the body to prove it!

He's an explorer, always has been. As a toddler we never knew where we'd find him--under the bed, in the closet, down in the basement. He loved to play hide and seek, a game we all quickly tired of.

"You go hide, Mattie," Heidi would instruct. "I'll come and find you in a minute." She never did look for him. She let him hide for three days once!

One of the things that really annoyed me about "the boy", is the fact that he loved to touch things, especially things that weren't his to touch--like my angel collection for instance, or his sister's books or his dad's tools. If you brought something new into the house, Matthew had to be the first one to finger it. It seemed to me that when he was growing up, everything he touched would self-destruct --thus his first words, "oh oh." Of course, anything he broke was never his fault.

"I didn't do it. It's not my fault." How many times have we parents heard those words?

Having an older sister, Matthew had to play a lot of "girl" games, but he lived through it and grew into a fine, young man, one not afraid to show his sensitive side. He likes women and I'm proud to say knows how to treat them. I think Bill and I did a good job raising a son. Bill taught him things a man needs to know--how to change the oil on his car, the art of belching--well, you know what I mean. I taught him how to cook, clean and do his own laundry. He'll make some woman a great husband some day, but I hope it's not to soon. After all, he is my baby.

Team players

"A good team player never takes sides." C. Hawkins

Summer is a great time to be outdoors, except when it comes to yard work. There's no doubt in my mind that my kids have allergies. It's evident when it comes time to do team yard work. They cough. They sputter. They splash water in their eyes until they finally realize that no one is paying attention. If you have allergies--use an inhaler and get on with life! That's my motto.

Heidi was the smart one. When we ask her to mow the lawn, she ran over her dad's bird feeder, nearly tipping herself over, destroyed my flower bed and cut the top off a struggling pine sap, all in one day's work. We never asked her to cut the grass again!

Matthew wasn't so lucky. He started cutting the grass and snow blowing the driveway around age eleven. It's still his job today, even though he's moved out!

Our kids were great game players. Heidi had Memory mastered by the time she was three years old and Matthew could beat anybody at Candyland. He was a sore loser when it came to the game, Sorry. No one would play with him because he was such a poor sport and cried everytime he was sent back to the start.

Heidi loved to make up her own games. Card Shop was her favorite. We saved every card we ever got just for this occasion. She'd spend hours sorting cards and lining them up in the middle of the living room floor. Somehow she would talk her brother into being the customer. The problem was, by the time she got the cards arranged into neat little piles he lost interest.

"You're not a team player," she would shout at him.

While most kids played house or cowboys and Indians, mine played church. All the dolls and stuffed animals became parishioners, except for one, tall, skinny monkey, Monk, dubbed "pastor." Because he most resembled our hippie pastor at the time. He was manipulated by Heidi. Matthew and a bright purple, roly poly monkey played the part of our Minister of Music, adored by both our children. As far as Matthew was concerned, it was his job to sing and play the pots and pans anytime he felt like it.

"Thou shalt not interrupt the sermon! It's a commandment of the Lord," Heidi would tell her brother, who was always asking forgiveness from the tall, skinny monkey for one thing or another. Matthew only sang and banged louder when his sister complained.

"Jesus loves you, but he loves me better," Matthew would sing as loud as he could, strumming on an old plastic dime store guitar we bought for a quarter at a rummage sale.

"Don't sing so loud!" Heidi demanded. "It hurts God's ears!"

"You can't tell me what to do," Matthew shouted back. "I'm in charge of music and me and Pastor Purple Monkey like it loud."

"Well, shut up, it's time for my sermon."

"It's not nice to say 'shut-up' in church," Matthew reminded his sister. "It's against the rules."

I'm not surprised that Matthew is our musical one. Although they both took piano lessons for two years, it's "the boy" who sits at the piano making his own music. (Mom's prodigy--I've been writing songs and stories since I was 10).

I remember my mother's rule of thumb when I wanted to take accordion lessons. "Piano first," she said. After two years of struggling with Chop Sticks she let me get an accordion, which I banged away on for seven years! Matthew went from the piano to a keyboard, to a $300 guitar that he dropped on the basement floor and cracked. He's outgrown those pots and pans. Now he's thinking drums! I'll be glad when he gets his own place and can annoy someone else besides his mother with his constant banging.

Heidi can pick out *Twinkle Twinkle Little Star*, the extent of her musical ability. She prefers to listen, to clap and to encourage others, probably a good thing. But both are excellent writers and were making up stories at an early age. Their penmanship, however, is another story.

Let me rephrase that. Both of my children grew up! Seriously, they have grown into respected adults.

Heidi graduated from Central Michigan University and is a social worker. She lives in Farmington Hills, Michigan and is doing quite well for herself.

Matthew is studying Criminal Justice at our local community college. He wants to be a policeman when he grows up, but who knows for sure, it changes every day! I'll support whatever career path he should chose and let him know that I am proud of him.

My children have inspired much of my writing and for that, I am thankful.

When I grow up

"When I grow up," said Matthew who is three, "I want to be a great big tree."

"Don't be silly," his sister said. "You cannot be a tree--you have to be what people be."

Matthew frowned, his eyebrows down.

"You could be a ballerina, or maybe a cook, or better still," his sister said, "you could work in a library and take care of books."

"Those aren't fun things for a boy like me to be. I'd rather be a bumble bee. Buzz buzz, or a monkey hanging from a tree."

"Matthew. Matthew. Matthew. Little boys cannot be monkeys swinging from a tree or bumble bees or flowers or trees. They have to be what people be. I know what I want to be," his sister said.

"What?" he asked.

"A mother," she said as a matter of fact. "What do you think of that?"

"I'd rather be a fireman and wear a bright, red hat! Hey, I think that I shall be a hat--a cowboy hat! What do *you* think of that?" His sister shook her head.

"Or," said Matthew, "I could be a fire truck and make a clanging noise. Clang. Clang. Bang. Bang. Look out!"

"Matthew! Boys cannot be fire trucks, so stop that noise," his sister said. "It hurts my head."

"A hat. A cat. A bee. A tree. I have to be what people be," Matthew sang as loud as only a boy could.

"You make a hurt inside my head. I think that I shall go to bed. When we grow up," his sister said, "we can worry then about what to be. For now, you are you and I am me, and that's the way it should be."

"I suppose," Matthew said, "but I'd rather be a tree that bends --and that's the end!"

My goal in life as a mother, anyway, is to help my children grow up, get them safely married and earning a respectable living so they can take care of me when I'm old--or at least take me out to lunch once in awhile.

I have to admit when Heidi got her first paycheck she did offer to take me out to lunch. I suggested a fast food place, but she wanted a "real" restaurant, our favorite Italian place where we go for special occasions. The food was more expensive than she thought it would be so we shared a plate. The bill came to $7.59. She only had $5 to spend so I had to loan her $2.95 plus tip money.

Matthew on the other hand played it smart. He took me out for a 39 cent burger at Hot N Now. Oh, I got a glass of water, too.

"Put extra ice in it," Matthew told the clerk. "Nothing's too good for my mom!"

Not unlike Matthew, where Heidi is generous to a fault, he's conservative, especially when it comes to his money. When they were small, B.J. (before jobs), I would give them each $50 to spend at Christmas. This money was meant to buy gifts for Mom and Dad, sister and brother, friends, etc. Heidi was an assiduous shopper. She would walk the malls for days until she found just the right gift for just the right amount of money. Matthew, however, would go into a discount store and look for dollar trinkets, hairpins or cheap costume jewelry for the women in his life, socks for dear old Dad (or food treats), baseball cards (one each) and bubble gum for friends! The rest of the money he'd pocket and spend on himself! It took longer than a few years to teach him that it's more blessed to give than to receive. I think he's finally got it as he's very generous now. Come to think of it, for the past three Christmases and for my birthday last year, I got paperback books. No matter. I love to read so it's always the perfect gift as far as I'm concerned. I just wish he would check my library first to see what I already have!

Both of my children are rather generous when it comes to the special people in their lives--I'm talking about the boyfriend/girlfriend and/or best friends. Christmas, birthdays, Easter, Valentine's Day-- even Halloween. The sky's the limit when it comes to giving gifts.

Heidi is very cautious in relationships. While Matthew falls in and out of love with every girl he meets. That scares me. Who knows maybe someday, I'll end up with the perfect daughter-in-law or son-in-law--or maybe not. With her expensive tastes, I just hope Heidi marries a rich man. Why not? A rich man is just as easy to love as a poor man. And besides, when the "goo goo-gagas" wear thin, you can always travel! Of course, with all the car repair bills she has, a garage mechanic would be a good choice, too.

When it comes to matters of the heart, a mother's best bet is to butt out. I learned that the hard way. It doesn't matter who they bring home, if I like them, they don't. The ones I think will make good mates--they let get away. Go figure.

Ironic, most of Matthew's good friends are women and Heidi's are men. In fact, her best friend in college was a guy. Good thing she's friend's with his wife, as well. (I hope they buy a book).

"I like men," Heidi says. "I find they are easier to talk to and much easier to work with than most women. They are not as petty." She and her new best friend, also male, seem to be inseparable. They're not dating, just going out. What's this "going out, but not dating" thing all about, anyway? Call me old-fashioned, but who better to marry than your best friend?

"Butt out, Mother."

Stuck on, "men are easier to talk to" I roll all consuming eyes. They may be easier to talk to, but are they good listeners? I have yet to find a man who really listens when a woman speaks. (My kids haven't been dating all that long; they still have much to learn.) I mean, how much do men really understand with their heads behind a newspaper or their eyes glued to the TV or computer screen?

One grunt and a nod means my husband actually heard me.

Two grunts and no nod means he has no idea what I'm talking about.

"I don't understand you, Woman," my husband complains. "There's no pleasing you. No matter what I say or do, it's usually wrong."

Exactly.

But the truth of the matter is, it's not that hard to please a woman. All we want is some quality time, some undivided attention, and a little love and romance. (In other words we don't want to share our men with the TV). A candlelight dinner and flowers for no reason once in a life time would be nice, and a man who listens once in awhile. A box of chocolates wouldn't hurt, either. And men--friend or lover--don't forget Valentine's Day!

I'm no expert, but one thing I know for sure, a man who forgets his 25th Wedding Anniversary is in big doo doo, probably until eternity!

"I didn't forget our 25th," Bill reminds me. "I bought you a $3 card and offered to take you to your favorite restaurant. Price was no object."

Just so you know, Burger King is not my favorite restaurant. And a $3 card--what is that?

Men! Can't live with them, can't live without them How many times have we women said that?

Kids, listen to your mother! If I had listened to mine, I'd still be single! But then, who would I make arts and crafts for, bake cookies for (when I bake) and for goodness sakes, I'd have no one to give motherly advice to that no one takes, anyway. And, I wouldn't have anything or anyone to write about. I wouldn't have a life!

Working at home--fun or frenzy?

"An ounce of work is worth many pounds
of words." St. Francis DeSales

Sometimes I hate working out of my home. I've been doing it now for years, believe me, it's no picnic. Long hours, 50 interruptions a day, pets to feed, laundry to fold, mail to collect. And don't forget to start the evening meal! Worse, is the millions of phone calls I get asking me, "What are you doing?" When I tell people I'm writing, they say, "Oh, that," and continue talking as if I have nothing else to do but to sit with the phone glued to my ear for two hours.

Why is it no one takes you seriously when you work at home? If I worked in a corporate office downtown with florescent lighting and a bottled water cooler, would someone call me and ask me, "What 'ya doing?" Would they ask me to stop at the cleaners during my lunch hour and pick up their dry cleaning? I think not.

"Well, you don't exactly work for a big city newspaper, you're running a tiny independent publication, how much work can that be?"

Believe me, it's a lot of work. Some days I'm at the computer before the sun comes up. Just because I'm not involved in corporate staff meetings doesn't mean I have time to wipe a runny nose every two minutes, fix a gourmet dinner or help my neighbor chase down her lost pet pig.

The President works at home, so does his wife. Does the President have time to sit and chit chat with friends in the middle of trying to run the country? Does anyone call the First Lady and ask, "Are you busy?" I don't think so.

Of course, I'm busy, I'm running a newspaper. I'm the editor and chief, head salesperson, in charge of accounting, public relations, news gathering and distribution. What do you mean, am I busy? If you don't believe me, there's still a half eaten donut gone stale lying on my desk. I haven't had time to eat it. I think it's been there for a week now.

My office is like Grand Central Station. If the phone isn't ringing off the hook, my husband or children are yelling, "What's for supper?" Do I care? I'm in the middle of a front page revelation!

The best advice I can give you about running a home business --locate your office in the bathroom! It's the one place in the house you can go without interruption--except at our house. When it's my turn to go, without fail, someone's banging on the door, asking, "Is it my turn, yet?"

"Yes! And it's your turn to cook supper, wash dishes, clean the sinks, mop the floor and feed the cat, and if you have any time left over you could help me run this newspaper!"

Working at home, fun or frenzy? Don't ask me, I haven't figured it out!

The Accent - 1995

Back to School

"Periods of tranquility are seldom prolific of creative achievement. Mankind has to be stirred up."
Alfred North Whitehead

All summer long kids run in and out. Windows rattle and doors bang.

In the middle of every day you hear, "Mom, there's nothing 'ta do. Can I make Kool-aid? Can we go across the street to play? Can Billy come over? Mom, Matt's in the pool with his shoes on again."

For three long months, you have a headache!

And then, late August--it suddenly appears rambling down the road over a sunbathed horizon--at last, the big yellow school bus!

Even though my children are grown now, I still remember the fury of that first day back to being sane again. It's like running a marathon, at least it was at our house...we can't find the shoes bought only two days ago. Book bags, school supplies and lunch boxes--all have mysteriously disappeared.

I can still picture in my mind sorting for an hour to find just the right pair of socks. Last minute teeth checks, brushing hair and handing out lunches squashed into brown paper bags (because no one can find the lunch boxes), giving a final shove out the door just in time--the bus is tooting at the driveway.

I know what it's like to breathe a heartfelt sigh of relief, to sit at the breakfast table drinking that first unspilled, unshared glass of fresh-squeezed juice in weeks, thinking--how wonderful, how beautiful, how peaceful tranquility is.

Then suddenly, a soft, little voice cries out, "Mom, I lonely. I got nothing 'ta do."

A smile, faint but nevertheless a smile, spreads over my face.

"Can I have Kool-aid?"

"Not for breakfast," I gently remind my three-year old wondering if it's too late to enroll him in preschool.

"Mom, read a book," he points to the shelf. "Play blocks."

The beautiful, peaceful tranquility of my morning slowly slips away, gone until the next stolen moment.

Even though my children are young adults now, off doing their own thing, I still find myself living on stolen moments. Each minute spent with them more precious now than when they were small, for I know it won't be long and they will be living on stolen moments, raising children of their own. Back to school or on to college, I think God meant for mothers to live in a world of stolen but precious moments--I wouldn't have it any other way!

School daze

"Education is kind of begetting." Lichenberg

When you stop to think how much an education cost these days, how can you bear to throw out anything remotely related to those good old school days?

I still have Matthew's first report card inside of his notebook binder and Heidi's first spelling book! I think my mother still has my first pair of saddle shoes! After all, you paid for that stuff a hundred times over!

Parents are forced to live at poverty level just so they can send their kids to the best schools. And isn't it odd, that the kid who dressed like a bum for 12 years now suddenly needs money for an "in" wardrobe which consists of baggy jeans with holes in the knees and an oversized tee shirt! As parents we had to learn terms like grunge, preppy, country--who knows what's in and what's out these days?

There is no such thing as a free education. The history book you thought was included in the price of an education ends up costing you $15 because "Somebody ripped it off--right out of my locker!" our son explains. Who would do such a thing?

The price of hot lunch, more thrown out than eaten, rises every year. Then, there's gym and locker fees, club fees, tickets to the football game, dance tickets, $3 for the favorite teacher's--what's her name, again? Christmas gift. And what about the bus driver? Shouldn't we get him or her something? After all, if anybody deserves a little recognition, it's probably the bus driver. They have to put up with 30 plus kids on a crowded bus, all talking at once, every day, all day long! Aspirins--that would be a good gift. Maybe we should just give them money; they'll probably end up in an early retirement home!

"Mom, I need \$20 to get my denim jacket cleaned."

"And why is that?"

"Because some idiot drew pictures all over it with an ink pen during fourth period."

"Great." I'm trying very hard at this point not to lose my cool. But I'd sure liked to take that ink pen and jam it...well, I won't go there. I suppose paying a dry cleaning bill is cheaper than buying a new coat or a new pair of Nikes because somebody stole yours in gym class. I'm still trying to figure out, why were the Nikes off the feet, again?

Expenses go up as the kids get older. There's the formal dress for homecoming. When I went to homecoming, the girls wore skirts and sweaters; the boys wore--whatever. Now, homecoming is practically a prom.

"Speaking of prom," my daughter says, "I need a new dress."

"What's wrong with the one you wore last year?"

"Mother, get real. I can't be seen in last year's prom dress! What would people say?"

"They'd probably say, 'there goes a sensible mom.'"

Graduation and all the expenses that go with it follow prom, not to mention college application fees. Now there's a rip off. The list of expenses goes on and on.

Before you donate money for Senior Send-Off, you'd better make darn sure your senior is going someplace!

The next thing you'll hear is, "Mom, I need a car!"

"Get a job! And that's my final answer!"

Cleaning--one of life's gambles

"Life has only one real charm--the charm of gambling.
But what if we do not care if we win or lose?"
Charles Brudelaire

Why is it so difficult to get anyone to clean out their closets? I know it's a gamble, but it has to be done. I'm the master cleaner at our house. I'm constantly cleaning. When I clean, I clean everything from top to bottom, from toilets to closets. Worse than closets are the johns--no will touch them. Why is it they can pee in 'em, but they can't clean 'em? And how come mothers are the only ones who can clear the kitchen table, run water in the sink, wash a dish, clean out a refrigerator and scrub the ceramic tile down? I have been pondering these questions since the day I got married.

"I'm not cleaning my closet," Matthew whines. "It's spooky. Things might be growing in there," he argues.

"My closet's got too much stuff in it to clean," Heidi complains. She's a pack rat, like her dad. The last time I sent her to room to thoroughly clean it, she was in the 10th grade and she was in there a week! All she threw out were some cutouts. She cried about it for a week.

"You never liked playing with cutouts," I reminded her.

"It doesn't matter," she sobbed. "They were little paper people."

When I send Matthew to clean up his room, he throws everything into his closet. He used to shove everything under his bed, but then we bought him a water bed and he couldn't do that anymore. His room looks like a pig sty most of the time. I've seen pig pens cleaner than my son's room!

"Hey, I resent that," a friend told me once. He raises pigs and says they are actually very clean animals. In fact he has a pet pig who lives in his house. Yuk! Now that's a scary thought. It's bad enough to have a cat living in the house. Animals are supposed to live outdoors in little coops or in the basement.

"Hey, wait a minute!" Matthew protests. "My room is in the basement."

"Exactly my point. Now clean your room before I call the exterminator!"

"What are you doing?" I ask my daughter rummaging through my closet.

"I'm looking for a notebook."

"I don't keep them in the closet anymore."

"Why not?"

"There isn't room."

"I can see why. Why are you saving this baseball trophy? Mattie was only in little league one season, and he wasn't even very good. Look, his trophy says, 'Most valuable player way out in the field...' And what are you saving these old report cards for, anyway? Matt's rubber worms...my old dolly, her eyes are missing for gosh sakes...and kites. We'll never use this stuff again. Whose college catalogs are these?"

"Mine," I admitted.

"They're yellow. You haven't been in college in..."

"Don't go there," I caution. "They have sentimental value."

"Mom, clean your closet."

"I will," I promise.

"When?"

"When the time is right."

"When will that be?"

"There is never a right time," I say.

"Exactly my point," Heidi agrees.

It's a gamble, but maybe someday we'll all clean our closets!

Note: Our closets finally got cleaned when we built a new house and moved!

Aging, a matter of mind

"Age will not be defiled" Francis Bacon

I'm having another birthday. At fifty something they seem to come faster then they used to! I read somewhere that age is a matter of mind. If you don't mind, it doesn't matter! Truthfully, the only time age didn't matter to me was when I was a kid. I could hardly wait for a birthday, then. I was even excited about it.

When you're young you think about aging in terms of fractions. When you're four and someone asks you how old are you? You never say I'm four going on five. You're more likely to say, "I'm four and a half." No one ever says they are 36 and a half going on 37!

When I was a teenager, I always jumped to the next number when someone would ask my age. I just turned 15, but I was going to be 16, soon. Even when I was 13, I was going to be 16. Well, I was going to be 16 eventually!

Ever notice when you're a kid, age 10--you can't wait to be a teenager so you can stay up past 9:00, and when you're 13, you want to be 16 so you can drive. Then comes that great day when you become 21. You don't turn 21--you "become" 21!

Then, you turn 30. What's that about? Makes you sound like bad milk--you "turned" 30. Then you're pushing 40. I hated the thought of it. Even the sound of "40" seemed old to me. I vowed not to move past 30 and suddenly, I was 40 so then I vowed I would stay 40 forever, but before I knew it I had reached 50. That was a dreadful time for me. I think I hid in my room for a week.

Now I wonder, will I make it to 60? And if I do, what will I be doing with my life? They say by age 60, you've built up so much speed in aging that you just "hit" 70 without even realizing it. After that, it's a day by day thing. Most people in that 70 age bracket are just glad to "hit" Wednesday!

My dad's 85. He says when you get to be 80 your happy to "hit" lunch! "Heck," he says, "you're glad when you hit 4:30."

People in their 80s don't make any long-term plans. They just live from day to day and are happy to be here.

My mother is 75. She says at this stage in life you are on borrowed time. She won't even buy green bananas. Who knows if she'll be around long enough to see them turn yellow! I'm betting she will.

It doesn't matter what stage you are in life, aging is a concern. Ever notice when someone reaches 90--time for them starts to go backward. They begin to tell people, "I was just 92 last week." Like 92 isn't all that old. If you're lucky enough to make it to 100, a strange thing happens, you become a kid again. I'm 100 and a half," you hear yourself saying.

I'm not sure I want to live to be 100. I mean, what would I do with myself? I'll probably still be writing. I guess when it comes right down to it, God has aging under control. It says so in Ecclesiastics, chapter three. "There is a an appointed time for every event under heaven." Even my birthday! Age doesn't really matter. After all, it's just a number and if it does matter, it's only because you let it.

The Crossroads - April 2000

(Internet friends contributed to this article)

The dreaded call

"We are terrified by the idea of being terrified."
Nietzache

There are three calls every mother dreads. The hospital, the police and the Elvis Presley Wedding Chapel in Las Vegas! I can well imagine the conversation...

"This is the Elvis Presley Wedding Chapel, Ma'am. Congratulations, your son just married a hitchhiker biker named, Tootise. The wedding went well...thank you, thank you very much."

Just the thought of a side-burned preacher dressed as the "king" singing, *Let me be your Teddy Bear* as the wedding theme song sends chills up and down my spine. The dire "Mom, I'm getting married" call so far has only happened in my dreams, but I know somewhere, I don't know where or when, it will happen.

The call that should have come from the police came from my son's girlfriend's parents at 9:00 on a Thursday night.

"Matthew's ok," the conversation began.

"What happened?" My husband took the call, probably a good thing; he's more rational when it comes to emergencies than I am.

"There's been an accident," the voice on the other end of the phone said.

Bill's grip on the receiver tightened. "How bad?"

The boy totaled his car," my husband spit out the ghastly words the minute I stepped foot in the kitchen. I had been to a bridal shower thinking all was well in my world. What a dote! All is never well when you're raising children.

"Is he ok?" I asked.

"Some bumps and bruises, but otherwise I guess he's ok."

"You guess?"

No mother wants to hear that "you guess" the boy is ok. She wants to know 100 percent, no doubts that her boy is up and running. She wants particulars.

"How bad is it?" I knew I shouldn't ask.

"It's bad," Bill said. "You don't want to see the car."

Wrong thing to say.

"I want to see the car," I said. "Now."

When I saw the Sunbird, purchased in July, wrecked in August, I was shocked. The trunk was shoved into the back seat which was now nonexistent. The passenger's side looked as if it had been bulldozed into the driver's side. Every window and mirror was broken. A roller blade was hanging out from what once was the trunk. The only part of the car that was actually in tact was the spot where Matthew had been sitting. There was no doubt in my mind that an angel had been riding shotgun that night. Bill was right. I didn't want to see the car!

The second call came a year and a half later during an ice storm. Matthew and the Chavalier did a $3,000 dance with a tree-- the tree won! It's a good thing the current girlfriend's father owned a body shop. And let's not forget the time he sideswiped a neighbor's mailbox on an icy road and put the Ferrio in the ditch.

"The wind did it!" he said.

Of course it did.

"He's a boy," my mother said remembering the perils of raising her own four males. "Boys are accidents waiting to happen."

I think she's right.

I'm not sure what's worse, the call from the police or the one from the hospital, or the dreaded note, in eligible handwriting, left on the kitchen table, most of which you'd need a handwriting expert to read.

Mom,

in case your wondering why this is so sloppy, it is because of the knife at Wendy's that hought it would be long and try and kill me.

Don't worry

because I told them I was a diabetic. I'm o.k. I t only hurt a little.

Blood, guts and gore! A knife...killed? A mother wants details! Whose blood? What knife? Who did what to whom? And where was the boy? A quick call to the clinic. No one knows anything about a young kid being brought in. Next, a call to his employer.

"Yes, Matthew had an accident," a squeaky young voice on the other end of the line confirms. "No, Mrs. Hawkins, I don't know how bad it is...he had to have sutures. I'm sorry, that's all I know."

Was my son living or dead? Did anyone know? Did anyone care? A fearful mother wonders these things. A hour later the boy finally calls.

"Hi Mom, it's me..."

"Where are you?"

"I'm at Angela's...didn't you get my note?"

"It wasn't much of a note," I say. "Are you ok?"

"There was a lot of blood, but I think I'm ok, now."

"You think? What happened?"

"It was on the note," he says.

"Yeah, right."

"I cut my finger," he says, "but I still got nine left!"

"That's not funny, Matthew."

"Don't worry, I only needed three sutures. We tried to call you, but we couldn't reach you. My boss took me to the Redi-Med Clinic...you'll never guess who operated on me?"

Operation? Sutures? Did I want some young punk of an intern or horrors, a med student with hardly any experience, sewing up my kid? Or worse, some old guy wearing thick glasses who should have retired five years ago? I don't think so!

"Did I tell you I tried to call? I'm feeling dizzy, Mom. I'll talk to you when I get home."

Click. The phone goes dead. Wait a minute! I wasn't done talking. Matthew finally arrived home three hours later, his finger all bandaged up. He recovered. I didn't.

Our daughter was not exempt when it came to accidents. Her first driving experience was the riding lawn mower. She backed into her dad's bird feeder an nearly killed the birds! I can still see Bill running after the lawn tractor pointing and yelling, "The feeder...the feeder."

Heidi couldn't hear a thing. She was bee bopping, headphones jacked up as loud as they would go--her music would drown out a tornado! We never asked her to mow the lawn again after that near calamity. Now that I think about it, she may have planned it that way!

The dreaded call from Heidi came at 7:30 in the morning. I had just gotten everyone safely, (or so I thought) off to school, and was about to go back to bed for a long winter's nap when the phone rang. I wondered as I sprang from my bed with a clatter--now what's the matter?

"Mom, it's me...Betsy's in the ditch!"

"Are you sure?" I groped for the night light.

"Of course, I'm sure. I know when a car is in the ditch."

"Are you ok?"

"I think so."

"Is the car ok?"

"It's stuck in a snowdrift in the ditch, how ok can it be?" Can you come and get me and take me to school?"

"No, I can't come to get you! You can't just leave your car stuck in a drift in the ditch!" By now I am fully awake thinking this day is not going well.

"Why not?" She says, "it's white--no one will notice."

"You have to call a wrecker."

"I don't know how to call a wrecker."

"Heidi you're in high school now, I'm sure you've mastered the art of dialing a phone...you can call a wrecker, they'll get you and Betsy out of the ditch so you can be on your way. Where are you now?"

"I'm at Lisa's house."

"And what does Lisa's father have to say?"

"He says I should call a wrecker."

"Sounds like a plan," I agree.

"Ok, I'll do it," she says.

A few minutes later the phone rings again.

"I don't seem to have my proof of insurance..."

It was at this point I deemed my day was not going to improve.

The second call came while Heidi was in college.

"Mom, it's me. I sort of had an accident."

"How does one sort of have an accident?" I politely asked.

Well, it's actually not an accident, just sort of an accident."

Sort of--that word again. "It's not? What exactly is it, then?" My curiosity had definitely peaked at this point in our conversation.

"It's more like a fender bender."

A fender bender. What happened?" I'm thinking two, three hundred dollars worth of damage--after all, she did say it was a fender bender and obviously, the girl was ok.

"It's what didn't happen."

"Ok," I say. "What didn't happen?"

"Well," she hesitates. "The truck in front of me stopped."

"And?"

"Bonnie didn't."

Bonnie was the second car. Why do women give their cars names, anyway? It's a mystery that has plagued mankind since the invention of the Lady Ford.

"Some joker in a red pickup slammed on his brakes at the light on Mission."

"Was the light per chance, red?"

"It was yellow the last time I looked," she defended. "He had plenty of time to make it through the intersection."

"But he decided to brake instead?"

"Exactly," she says. "Two cars could have made it."

"But two cars didn't make it," I affirmed. "One ran into the other."

"I'm sure I braked. Next thing I know, I'm staring into this guy's taillights. His truck needed a wash job," she added as if that would justify spending hundreds of dollars on repair bills.

"If you stopped, how is that you happened to rear end a pickup, a bright red one at that?" I wanted to know.

"It wasn't red," she said. "It was more maroon. I stopped, but something must have happened."

"Like what?"

"Bonnie had a sudden burst of energy and then thrust forward. That's when I rammed into the truck. There wasn't much damage to the truck. The guy driving was really nice about it; he was kind of cute for an old guy. He didn't even put in an accident report, Mom. Wasn't that nice of him?"

"Very nice," I agreed. "What about your car, how much damage does it have?"

"Hardly any, the hood is pushed in a bit that's all."

"How much is a bit?"

"I'm sure financially speaking, there's hardly any damage."

Wrong. That so-called fender bender and Bonnie's new paint job cost us $2,000! And two years later, the paints chipping!

I don't want to admit this, confessing such a thing could be a bad omen, but when it comes to accidents, I'm afraid my children take after their father. He has had his share of fender benders, believe me. I don't think he's owned a vehicle that he hasn't put a ding in. The blue pickup was hit twice in the same spot at the same intersection!

"Hi, Hon, it's me." This time the "me" was my husband. "I had an accident with the truck. I'm ok, but I'll be late getting home."

"What happened?" I met him in the driveway.

"Ah, some idiot hit me at the Kawkawlin intersection. I stopped. He didn't."

Where have I heard this story before? "I don't suppose the guy behind you had a sudden burst of energy and sort of just thrust forward?"

"What do you mean?"

"Never mind," I said. "It's a long story. How much damage this time?"

"Two grand," he said. "I already got an estimate. I'm taking it in next week."

Two weeks later, driving home from his favorite body shop (I'm sure considering the number of cars we own we've put a couple of the body man's kids through college by now), Bill was stopped at the same intersection when he was hit from behind, again!

You probably think I'm making this up--I'm not, scouts honor. We have too many of the real thing to fake an accident! Excuse me for interrupting this saga, but I should go lay hands on the new pickup before something happens to it!

Holidays--what's it all about, Alfie?

"I have great confidence in the revelations which
holidays bring forth." B. Disraeli

If there is ever a time that one might wish to be away at sea,
it's during the hassle of the everyday holiday. There are so many:
Easter, Thanksgiving, Valentine's Day, Halloween, Fourth of July,
All Saints Day, Lent, St. Patty's Day, Mother's Day/Father's Day,
Sweetest Day, Hanukkah, My Favorite Teacher Day, Back to School
Shopping Day (I'm sure it's a holiday for somebody), Birthdays--
and let's not forget the most important of them all--Christmas!

I don't dare end this book without mentioning a few favorite
holiday traditions and maybe some not so favorite. Not exactly sure
what it is I'm expected to say about these long-standing holiday
traditions that so many of us cherish in our hearts, I decided to enlist
the help of a professional--six-year-old Lynn.

"My name is Connie Hawkins, I'm a writer," I explain to Lynn.
"I'm writing about holiday traditions and sure could use your help.
Do you think maybe you could help me?"

"Maybe." Lynn shakes her head flailing blond curls in every
direction. "What's a tradition?" She wants to know.

"Well, it's something you do every year, that you really enjoy
doing, like baking Christmas cookies."

Lynn nods her head. I assume she understands my plight.

"Can you tell me about the first Thanksgiving?" I ask Lynn,
pencil in hand ready to take notes.

I quite enjoyed Lynn's version of the first Thanksgiving and
thought you might enjoy it, too.

The First Thanksgiving

The first Thanksgiving was a long, long time ago...before I was born, even. I think my grandma was there. It's a story about the pygmies coming to America on the Mayflower. "That was a bi--g boat," Lynn explains. Two other boats, the Pinto and the St. Marie crashed at sea--a whole bunch of pygmies were killed. The Mayflower finally landed on a rock. The pygmies were so happy they started to sing and dance, giving thanks--that was the first Thanksgiving. Except, I forgot the Indians.

See, the pygmies were so happy they finally landed their boat, they wanted to have a party with balloons and everything, but since half of the pygmies were dead they didn't have enough for a party so they decided to invite the Indians to dinner.

"Where did the Indians come from?" I wanted to know.

"Hm-m-m...I think they must have come from India. Maybe they came from Universal Studios...Lynn was in a deep state of befuddlement. The important thing is the Indians were there at the first Thanksgiving. They even bought corn. They all sat around eating cornbread and pudding--stuff like that. That was the end of the story.

What kind of Thanksgiving traditions do you celebrate at your house?" I ask.

"My mom cooks a big turkey."

"How big?"

"About 100 pounds, I think."

"Wow, that's a big bird. How long does it take to cook?"

"About 21 days!" Lynn says. "Mom dresses the bird before she cooks it."

"You mean like in a hat and scarf?"

Lynn giggles. "No, silly." She splatters it with mayonnaise and butter and puts soggy bread with onions and celery in the hole. When it's all cooked good, we eat it. Then we have my grandma's coconut cream pie and chocolate sauce for dessert."

"What about opening presents?"

Lynn wrinkles her nose. "We do that on Christmas. That's the holiday that comes about three days after Thanksgiving."

"Well, what do you do after you eat up all the turkey?"

"The men go into the den and watch stupid football. The ladies and girls, like me, have to wash up all the dirty dishes--there's a pile of them, too, a mountain tall. We make a wish on the turkey bone, too."

"What do you wish for?"

"You can't tell your wish, 'cause if you do, it won't come true."

"What about coloring eggs?"

Lynn giggles again. "You don't color eggs on Thanksgiving," she says. You color eggs on Easter," she smiles. I can tell she likes to color eggs.

This is a good time for me to tell Lynn about coloring eggs, not the antireligious custom many Christians view it to be, but rather spiritually significant.

"Did you know Easter eggs were a symbol of a belief in everlasting life, Lynn?"

"No, she says. "I didn't know that."

Not so strange a symbol when one considers that the egg holds within itself the beginning of new life. Ancient Persians believed that eggs laid during Easter Week were holy and would stay fresh for one year. A Creola Good Friday belief is that fish lay eggs on Good Friday and a rooster crows three times at 3 pm. A Ukraine custom states that orange, red, yellow and purple eggs were used to symbolize the passion of Easter, spring and new life; the most elaborately designed eggs in the world, given during the season of Easter, Ukrainian eggs are still offered as tokens of love during the Easter season.

Lynn begins to politely yawn. (This is a good place for you to take a break) while I rattle on. This is important stuff. Pysanky eggs have the words "Christ is risen" written on them, a tradition still very much alive in parts of Canada, at least that's what I've been told. And research seems to support that theory.

In Miles, New York, colored eggs serve as a reminder that Christ died, rose and lives again. Eggs are brought to the altar on Easter morning to be blessed. On Holy Saturday, some Polish congregations still bring baskets of eggs and other foods to the altar for a special blessing by the priest. These customs aren't so new. Ancient civilizations thought of the egg as holding the secret of new life. In India and Egypt, the world was said to have begun by the splitting of a huge egg. One-half became heaven and the other half earth.

Jewish congregations still use the egg in traditional Seder meals in celebration of Passover. An egg, hard-boiled then roasted on an open flame, recalls their mourning for the destroyed second temple. Today, the egg in many Jewish homes still symbolizes rebirth.

As Christianity spread, Christians coveted many of the pagan practices turning them into modern more acceptable rituals. Coloring eggs, Easter egg hunts, baskets filled with chocolate eggs and other goodies is now a tradition in many homes around the world.

"Eating an egg," said Oscar Wilde, "is always an adventure --each one different." Eggs, plain, ceramic, candied, chocolate, colored, blown out or painted are still considered an Easter keepsake, more important, they still symbolize new life!

I could see Lynn was not too impressed with my research on eggs. So I told her next time she goes on an Easter egg hunt do as Mark Twain instructed, "Put all thine eggs in one basket and then, watch thine basket very carefully."

"Who's Mark Twain? Was he a friend of the Easter Bunny?"

"Not exactly," I tell Lynn.

Speaking of bunnies...don't you just loath those Cadbury egg commercials? I really hate bunnies that cackle like a chicken!

Easter is the greatest religious festival of the year. As significant as the cross is, children still have Easter visions of their own dancing through their heads.

"Is there really a place for the Cadbury bunny among our Easter traditions? Kids thinks so. To prove my point, children ages 4 through 9 shared their opinions with me about Easter and Mr. E. Bunny in particular.

"He's busy as a bee, especially at Easter."

"My mother tried to get rid of the Easter bunny, once, but she couldn't go through with it."

"My mother tried to buy the Easter bunny off, but he's too smart for that."

"Chickens get a bum rap at Easter," one boy said. "I think since the Easter Bunny couldn't deliver eggs without help from his chicken friends, that the Easter Chicken should get more respect. What would happen if chickens refused to lay eggs, where would the Easter Bunny be then?"

"I think the Easter Bunny should deliver cheese. I like it better than eggs."

"Mrs. Hawkins, do you know why the Easter Bunny has such big ears?"

"No, Leo, I don't. Why does the Easter Bunny have such big ears?"

"All the better to hear with, my dear."

"That's not funny, Leo," Sara scolds.

"I don't get it?" Andy frowns.

"Me either," Leo admits. "My brother told it to me. He don't get it, either."

"Why don't we leave milk and cookies for the Easter Bunny?" I ask.

Everyone laughs, but no one has an answer.

"Seriously, we all know why we celebrate Easter, right?"

"It's about the cross," Lynn says. "And about Jesus dying on the cross for our sins. He was very brave."

"Why do you suppose he did that?"

"Because he loved us very much. We don't have to feel sad about it though, because he's not dead anymore."

"That's right," I said. "On the third day he rose from the dead and descended into heaven where he sits with God the Father."

"Waiting for us," Lynn adds.

"Amen," I say.

"Amen." The kids echo.

"What do you think about Halloween?"

"It's fun," most of the kids agree.

Some thought it was bad, but most of the kids agreed they enjoy dressing up in silly costumes and going door to door begging for candy.

"I like carving a pumpkin." Lynn says.

"That reminds me of a story about a pumpkin named Peter."

"Tell us about Peter." The kids begin chanting, "Peter. Peter, pumpkin eater..." but begin to quiet down as I start my story about a little pumpkin named Peter, a very unhappy pumpkin.

The Reluctant Pumpkin

Peter Pumpkin was not a very happy pumpkin. You see Peter hated Halloween and he hated being a pumpkin. Every year on the eve of Halloween, the boys and girls from Happy Hollow hurried out to the pumpkin patch to choose a jack-o-lantern for October 31st.

The first thing they did was pound and tap poor Peter's head --sometimes they'd even step on him and hurt him.

Once they decided on which pumpkin they wanted, in this case, it's Peter, they'd toss him into the back of a dirty, old pickup truck. Peter didn't like being in the back of that old pickup truck; he rolled around all the way home getting dents and bruises all over his beautiful, orange pumpkin shell.

Once home, the boy and girl who chose Peter began to carve holes in his body. (With help from grown-ups, of course).

"When they cut holes in me," a sad Peter said, "they throw away what's inside--my heart. Without a heart I cannot love, and I want so desperately to love all the boys and girls and to have them love me." A lone tear trickled from Peter's eye.

Peter hated it when folks carved him a mean looking face. It scared the little kids away and made them cry. Sometimes it made Peter cry, too.

"If only I could have a happy, smiling face, then I could let my love shine!" Peter said.

What can I do about this problem Peter thought to himself. *There must be something I can do to change.*

Peter tried to change. He disguised himself as a skeleton, an old woman, a black cat, even a scarecrow. But all those faces were more scary than his own. Peter was so unhappy he cried big pumpkin tears.

A boy dressed in a beggar's costume came along and saw Peter's sad face. "What's wrong Jack-o-lantern, why are you crying?" The boy asked.

"Being a Jack-o-lantern, that's what's wrong," Peter cried all the harder. "And my name is Peter Pumpkin, not Jack-o-lantern," he said. "I don't want to be a scary Jack-o-lantern, all I want to be is Peter the happy pumpkin--a pumpkin everybody can love."

Hearing Peter's sad story made the boy feel bad. "I think I can help," the boy said. He quickly turned Peter's frown upside down --now Peter was smiling!

"Thank you. Thank you!" Peter shouted with joy. "Now, at long last, my light can shine with love for all the world to see and I can truly be a happy pumpkin."

Heidi

Matt

I always hated Halloween, not because it was a good or bad day, but because I was the only one in my neighborhood who couldn't sew! A trait I shared with fellow writer, Erma Bombeck, who wrote about it in her book *Family--the ties that bind and gag.* Like me, Erma too, dreaded all those cute little trick or treaters coming up the walk, smiling and happy, wearing costumes that would make a mother proud. Except, it caused us to cringe.

You could always recognize my kids; they were the ones with paper sacks over their heads trying to figure out themselves who on earth they were supposed to be! Except for one year when Matthew, thanks to Aunt Gayle, came to the school party dressed as Mickey Mouse (he was so proud of that costume), and Heidi thanks, to Grandma Gerri, got to be a fairy princess. Otherwise, my kids went as the bag people!

One year I had to run a short errand and left Bill in charge of passing out candy. When I came home at 8:00 the porch light was turned off.

"You're out of candy, already?"

"Yep. Two big kids came, one dressed in baggy jeans with holes in them and a tee shirt down to his knees; he looked like a bum. The other kid had a jersey on, looked like a rejected football player."

"Those weren't trick or treaters," I said. "That was your son and his friend!" I scolded.

"Doesn't matter. I gave 'em all the candy and shut off the light. Halloween is over."

It seemed like a good plan to me. Pass out all the candy to the those who come to the door first then Halloween is over. Works for me.

It doesn't really matter how we choose to celebrate Halloween, as long as we remember that as Christians we are to be just like Peter Pumpkin, a light onto the dark that shines with God's love for all mankind.

There is a lot of controversy as to whether or not Christians should allow their children to participate in the pagan holiday of Halloween. Some say, it's no big deal. Others disagree, but I don't think you can disagree without first knowing the facts.

The American celebration of Halloween rests upon Scottish and Irish folk customs which can be traced from pre-Christian times. Although Halloween has traditionally became a night of celebration among young children, it's beginning was otherwise.

Earliest celebrations were held by the Druids in honor of Saman, lord of the dead, whose festival fell on November 1. It was the Druids' belief that at the end of the festival, Saman called together all the wicked souls, releasing them in the form of ghosts, spirits, witches and elves. The Druids, an order of priests in Ancient Gaul and Britain, also believed that the cat was sacred because it was once in human form. From these ancient stories came the present-day stories of witches, ghosts and black cats used in Halloween activities. Pagans believe that one night a year, souls of the dead returned to their original homes. To exorcise these spirits, one would set out a food treat. If you didn't, they would trick you by casting a wicked spell, thus the custom of "trick or treat."

It was the Celts who chose October 31 as their New Year's Eve, intended to celebrate anything wicked and evil, living or dead. The celebration remained until the Romans conquered the Celts in 43 A.D. The Romans added fruit and trees to the custom, thus the association of bobbing for apples. The apparently harmless lighted pumpkin face of "Jack-o-lantern" is an ancient symbol of a soul, named for a man called Jack, who could not enter heaven or hell. As a result, he was doomed to wander in darkness with his lantern until Judgement Day.

Fearful of spooks, folks began to hollow out turnips and pumpkins, placing lighted candles in them to scare away evil spirits. Satan worshipers still celebrate Halloween today.

Unsuspecting mothers, Christians and otherwise, pour millions of dollars annually into the purchase of Halloween costumes and candy each year thinking it's simply a fun day to celebrate. Fun? I was glad when we put all that nonsense behind us.

The Bible says we are to have no part in the deeds of darkness. Both Christians and Jews are forbidden (Deuteronomy 18:10-11) to participate in anything even remotely considered occult or witchcraft. Both are an abomination to God. I Thessolians 5:22 says, "Abstain from evil." The Apostle Paul speaking to believers at Ephesus told them, "give no place to the devil." (Ephesians 4: 27.)

No Christian would knowing glorify Satan, but perhaps we need to take a closer look at what "trick or treat and Halloween" really represent. Is it, in disguise as something fun and harmless, actually, a subtle attempt of the devil to plant his seeds of destruction? Christian youth want to have fun on this day, too. Here are some alternatives to celebrating Halloween the world's way: A harvest bake off. Kids can produce their own delectable holiday treats, creating innovative variations of pizza, party mix, peanut butter & jelly bars, pumpkin cookies, and caramel apples, all of which make delicious treats. The church could host a bake sale. The youth could have fun with their original creations and make money at the same time.

If baking isn't your forte, how about an old fashion hay ride, campfire, hot dog roast, sing-along or sixties party (with prizes for the best costume) or a treasure hunt? If your child insists on "trick or treating," suggest a positive, uplifting costume. Make sure they understand the rules of the road, wear reflective clothing and stick to familiar neighborhoods.

And remember, if you are as talented as I am at the sewing machine--there's always paper bags!

Luck or Promises?

The luck of the Irish, you hear that phrase a lot, especially in March as we prepare for St. Patty's Day. What does that phrase "luck of the Irish" really mean and just what kind of luck are we talking about?

For all accounts historically, persecution, political and religious unrest--it seems to me the Irish had more bad luck than good. I know what it's like to have bad luck. I sometimes think if our family didn't have bad luck, we'd have no luck at all!

On the other hand, when I think about it, as Christians, we really don't need to concern ourselves with luck, good or bad, because we can stand on the promises of God. The Bible is filled with His promises. Seek ye first the kingdom and you will find promises of grace, mercy, peace, rest, forgiveness, freedom from the cares of this world.

The most important promise, the hope of eternal life is found in one of the most quoted scriptures in the Bible, John 3:16: "For God so loved the world, he gave his only son that whosoever believes in Him shall not perish but have everlasting life."

Luck, or promises of God? I'll stand on the promises anytime!

The Accent - March 1995
The Crossroads - March 2001
Revised for this publication

With so many holidays, we often get so caught up in celebrating, that we forget to focus on what's really important. In some religious circles it doesn't seem to have much credence anymore, but as a kid I remember celebrating Lent, a time of prayer and fasting. I wasn't Catholic so I didn't do the Ash Wednesday thing, but many of my friends did. I always felt like I was missing something because I didn't start the season of Lent with the administration of ashes to my forehead, a reminder of man's mortality. According to the Catholic faith, ashes are a sign of penitence. Traditionally a time of preparation for baptism into the Christian faith at the Easter vigil on Holy Saturday. Other denominations view lent as a symbol of new life, using those 40 days preceding Easter as a time of self-examination, a time to reflect on Jesus and the cross. As a stumbling people, we certainly need more time for self-examination and reflection on spiritual things.

During Lent, some churches use different colored crosses to represent the different aspects of Christ's suffering at Calvary. The Hunter's Cross shows the betrayal and arrest of Jesus. The Crusaders' Cross has a focus on the passion of Christ. Cross of the Accent is the cross that leads to Calvary with emphasis on faith, hope and love. The Arched Cross expresses ultimate healing, while the Lorraine Cross, a symbol of World War II showing the French Resistance, speaks of contingency in the midst of change. The Cross of the Sovereign spotlights the trial of the King of Kings. I don't think my kids know what Ash Wednesday is, what ashes symbolize, or what meaning Lent holds for them personally.

As a kid, I was always fascinated with Judaism and Hanukkah. I don't know why. I only knew one little girl who was Jewish and that was in mere passing, but she always seemed so dedicated to her faith. I guess that's what I admired most about her. She taught me a couple of Hanukkah songs and how to play dreidal games. It wasn't until years later that I became friends with the rabbi and was even invited to his home once for a traditional Hanukkah meal of potato pancakes, (lattkas.)

Bill finally found someone he could talk to about the Old Testament. It was a most enjoyable evening, one I will always treasure. It gave me a deeper appreciation for the way others worship.

Advent, centering around the four Sundays preceding Christmas, is another holiday event I think many Christians ignore. I like Advent, and the anticipation of the coming of the Christ-child it symbolizes. In some churches, celebrating Advent includes lighting candles, another custom my children, sadly, know nothing about. The Advent wreath, the center of daily devotions in many Christian homes, represents God's eternal love. Each week a candle on the wreath is lit. The center candle reflects Christ as the "light of the world." Traditionally, Advent is a time when Christians focus on daily devotions, prayer and the coming of the Savior. Other advent traditions include: hanging banners in the windows of the church, displaying Advent logos, which symbolize how Advent starts in darkness, but ends in total light, decorating the Jesse Tree where each day symbols (crosses, hearts, lambs etc.) are hung on the tree to remind us of God's love. Kids make Advent cookies, and Advent chain links containing Biblical messages pertinent to the Advent season, which ends on December 25 with the celebration of Christmas, almost everyone's favorite holiday.

It's Christmas again, and I'm going home.
I'm not sure why I'm going home.
I think it's because Santa Claus, and
Christmas carols are meant to be shared
With those you love--so I'm going home.

In my youth as the holidays approached I would always try to visit a shut-in. One Christmas I called upon a frail old woman who lived in a nursing home. It was my intent to spread a little joy, and to bring her a Christmas surprise. It wasn't much, some lotion, and a box of candy, but it was a thought.

As soon as I entered the building, I saw just the lady I knew I was there to visit. She was sitting alone, off in a corner. No one paying her any attention. As I approached I noticed a tear in her eye.

"Why are you crying, dear saint?" I asked her. "What can I do to make your day better?"

"What happened," she whispered, "to the Christmas I used to know? Where are the children I sang sweet songs to? And shared my love and joy with? Where is my Christmas kiss?"

"I guess your family has grown, busy with lives of their own."

"Yes," she nodded, "no time now for an old woman in an old folks home."

"But, you're not alone." I gently reminded her. "Someone has come to give you this." I bent down and gave her a Christmas kiss.

A big smile spread across her wrinkled face. "It is you that has come?"

"Not I," I said, "but the Son. Jesus loves you, my friend."

Helping someone less fortunate, visiting the sick, the lost, the dying--doing good for someone else is a concept I tried to pass on to my own family during the holidays. When my children were small, we'd pick a family from the church and/or community and shower them, anonymously if we could, with gifts. My kids still remember those times as some of our best Christmases.

Christmas is a busy time. The baking, the feasting, the shopping, the wrapping, the card sending, decorating. I'm always glad when it's over. But, it isn't until I start taking down the decorations and am carefully wrapping the figurine of the baby Jesus in tissue paper to be put away for another year that my mind begins to focus one last time on the age-old story of the Nativity.

Suddenly, I realize it isn't the lights that brighten our homes at Christmas, nor is it the year-end feasts or even the Christmas colors of red and green that are important. These things aren't Christmas. No, not even the evergreen tree that becomes the center of attention for all these weeks, or the Advent wreath or the holly, or the Christmas carols we sing. None of these things make Christmas.

Christmas is a tiny little baby lying in a manger who came to save a dying world. In the awesomeness of God's greatest gift to us, it's almost a shame to hide that small figure away in a shoe box, not to think of the baby Jesus again for another year.

It seems to me what we really need is a little bit of Christmas all year.

The Bay City Times - December 1988

A new solution to the same old complaints

"Give power to my good resolutions--this request could
be part of the Lord's Prayer." G.C. Lichtenberg

Why is it the year always ends with the same old complaints,
only we call them resolutions--we make them and break them! I
think it's a mind game we play with ourselves.

Every year I vow to take old end-of-the-year complaints and
turn them into New Year solutions.

As the disciples traveled the road sharing the Good News of
the Gospel, they entered a house and gave it a joyous blessing, even
greeting one another with a holy hug and a kiss of love, spreading
peace and goodwill wherever they went.

Each January I vow to do the same, especially during the
holiday season. After all, the holidays are suppose to be happy times,
a time to be reunited with loved ones--no more of this, "you look
awful since I last saw you" stuff. Never mind that Aunt Suzy has
gained a ton of weight or that Uncle Louie's hair transplant failed.
(Bald is beautiful.)

"It's good to see you--you look great!" should be our response
every day of the year. As Christians, it's our job to exhort one another,
more so at Christmas, after all, 'tis the season to be jolly. I suppose
it would be a lot easier to deck the halls if certain children would
learn how to behave themselves (our own little angels excluded,
because after all they are always on their best behavior). Then again,
it would probably do us all well to become as a little child, (God
bless them every one) especially during the holidays.

Second on my list of resolutions is to get moms out of the
kitchen at holidays and into the festivity of things. Most moms slave
for days preparing a feast fit for a king, that no one seems to appreciate.
If she's lucky enough to get everyone around the table, it's usually
over grunts and grumbling--the turkey's too dry, the gravy's too thin

--dads want to make the meal quick so they don't miss the big game. The grandkids fight over the drumsticks, and the VCR. (You can't play video games when Grandpa's watching football. Why can't Grandma have two TVs like everybody else?)

No one seems to notice the beautifully set table, the gracious china (all the plates match), or the neatly folded cloth napkins. "Paper would have been easier," Aunt Gert grumbles, "no d--m (please, not in front of the children) dishes to wash!"

There's always someone unhappy with the meal.

"Yuk! What is this stuff?" The little ones ask.

"I'm on a fat-free, no-salt diet," say the seniors.

"I don't eat meat," says the vegetarian, "but the relish tray looks delicious!"

No matter what your complaint, almost everyone over-eats during the holidays, and there's never enough cheesecake.

That reminds me--dieting. It's at the top of everyone's New Year's resolution list around the world!

"Why did you let me eat so much?" is the number one gripe between spouses. Lack of self-control is really not the fault of the cook. Worse than overeating is the one who just picks--never mind that the lady of the house just spent three days cooking for your dining pleasure.

After dinner we really settle down. Over fed and just about fed up with family togetherness, it's time to tackle the huge mound of gaily wrapped presents in assorted sizes and shapes under the tree.

Next year, it's number four on my list, I'm going to remember batteries to go with that thing-a-ma-jig I bought Uncle Harry. I'm also definitely going to leave tags intact because ultimately someone will ask, "Can I exchange this?" And surely, someone will boldly exclaim, "What's this?" I love getting those gifts, myself.

I never could please my father-in-law. For twenty some years I knocked myself out trying to find something he would like. He returned everything we ever gave him. I guess he had everything he needed. At one point in our relationship, I had thought of saving my money and just giving him a hug! I had a feeling he probably needed a hug more than anything else we could have given him.

Once the gifts are opened and the living room floor is cluttered with paper, the kids start bugging you about wanting to go home. So much for those tangible symbols of thoughtfulness and love.

Something's amiss here. How can a season intended for peace, brotherhood and love end up such a disaster? I think I know the answer. It's also the solution to all those resolutions we make and break. The miracle of it is, it's guaranteed to work without batteries, no assembly is needed, and it lasts forever. You'll never outgrow it.

It's love, folks. Pure and simple. The scriptures are overflowing with it. Trouble is, it takes practice and it's hard work. Consequently, most people let their love grow cold. It's easy to love the lovable, the hard part is loving the not so lovable. Praying for your enemies and for those who persecute you is harder still.

But Christ said in the book of Matthew "...by this you will know my disciples, if you have love for one another..." Timothy instructs to love. In Corinthians we are told to pursue love and in II Peter it says to "greet one another in brotherly kindness and in Christian love, keeping ourselves in the love of the Lord at all times..."

Love is a gift from God. Without it, we are nothing more than a nosy gong or a clanging symbol. Love is the only thing that lives forever. The world and everything in it will pass away, but now abides faith, hope, love, but the greatest of these is, love. I am firmly convinced that love is the cure for what ails a dying world; it's the only solution to our same old resolutions. Next year, in spite of everything, I am vowing to have a pleasant and happy holiday. I am going to love until it hurts!

Bay City Times - January 1995

Midyear resolutions--a progress check

"Procrastination is the art of keeping up with yesterday."
Don Marquuis

Here's a few suggestions you might want to consider as a midyear review, or a progress check, if you will. They're guaranteed to make you a better person, no matter when you observe them. In fact, forget the word "resolution"--it's too late anyway. Think of these suggestions as your personal prayer to God. If you add "Dear Lord" at the beginning of the list, instead of midyear resolutions, you have a midyear prayer list:

Dear Lord, keep me from the habit of thinking I must say something on every subject ever written on every occasion.

Release me of the burden of trying to straighten out everybody's affairs. Sometimes it's ok to say "no."

Make me thoughtful, but not moody; helpful, but not bossy. Help me to strive for patience over irritability.

Keep my mind free of the recital of endless details. Help me to focus on that which is really important. Give me wings to get to the point.

Seal my lips of aches and pains. I'm getting older now, they are increasing, and my love of hearing about them is becoming sweeter as the years go by.

I ask not for improved memory, but a growing humility when my memory seems to clash with others.

Teach me the glorious lesson that, occasionally, I may be mistaken. Give me the ability to see the good things in the unexpected places and talents in unexpected people.

Lord, let me be a little bit kinder and a whole lot more loving in my thoughts, actions and deeds. And most important, let me be not afraid to shine for all mankind that I might brighten a corner in someone else's world.

The Accent - June 1966

On death and dying

"A well-spent day brings happy sleep, so
a life well used brings happy death."
Leonardo DaVinci

"There are only two things you have to do in this life, pay taxes and die." I don't know where that old saying came from or who said it, but I like it. I like the sound of it and the sense of it, especially the part about death--it's inevitable.

I dragged myself to the kitchen table one morning looking like death warmed over.

"What's wrong with you?" My daughter asked.

"I'm sick," I moaned, sputtering and coughing. "I think I've got pneumonia."

"You're always sick," she reminded me. "Last week you thought you had kidney disease. The week before that it was gout. It's always something with you."

The following Tuesday I marched into my doctor's office and belatedly announced, "I'm dying."

"And you know this because?"

"Headaches," I said, "suggestive of a brain tumor."

"Have you been reading those home medical books, again?" he asked, checking my heart and blood pressure.

"Maybe."

He hauled out one of those little flashlights doctors always seem to carry in their pockets and proceeded to look into my bloodshot eyes.

"When was the last time you had your eyes checked?"

"I can't remember," I sheepishly admitted.

"Say ah...throat looks good. Glands are a little swollen."

"Do you think it's lymph node cancer?"

"I think it's swollen glands. Hm-m-m, this could be a problem," he said, probing into my ear.

"Is it serious?"

"It's an infection," he relates. "I'm going to order some lab work and a hearing test, among others."

"A hearing test. Why? There's nothing wrong with my hearing. It's my head that hurts."

"I think there is. You never seem to hear me when I tell you there's nothing wrong with you."

"I get dizzy spells, and don't say I'm a dizzy dame--that's my husband's line."

"How long have you had these dizzy spells and the headaches?"

"A couple of weeks, maybe a month or so."

"Is the pain concentrated in one spot or does it move around?"

"I don't know...the headaches move around, but the dizziness is in one spot, my head."

"Very funny." He gives me an annoying look, which I ignore.

"I'm going to prescribe something for the ear infection."

"What about the dizziness...can I have some Antivert?"

He handed me two prescriptions. "Just in case you are dying, can I have an autographed copy of your book?"

I think he wanted a copy of my book because he knows once I'm gone I'll be rich and famous. What good is that going to do me if I'm dead?

I wonder if they have a newspaper in heaven? I could write the Heavenly News. Speaking of news I should write my own obituary. It'll probably be the last thing ever written about me. I want to make sure it's done right!

I should buy into a drug franchise I thought as I pulled my car into the parking lot of the drugstore. *I spend enough time here.*

"Hello, Mrs. Hawkins, nice to see you again." The pharmacist is unusually pleasant. Does he know something I don't?

I manage a polite smile. Considering how often I come in, you'd think we'd be on a first name basis. I knew it! He's looking at me funny. There is something wrong with me after all--I was sure of it!

On second thought, he probably thinks I'm a hypochondriac. Now, there's an idea, a hypochondriac who thinks she is dying--what a great character for a book, a TV movie even. Now let's see, who'd play my part?

Paying my drug bill is even more painful than paying my doctor bill. You know why they call the senior years, the golden years? It's because the pharmacist gets all your gold!

Thinking about the five novels already on the computer waiting for me to do something with, I suddenly realize I simply don't have time to die. I have books to publish!

"The world's dumb indifference makes you mad enough to keep on fighting". I read that somewhere, from my book of *Unusual Quotations,* I think. As for me, telling the world my troubles always seems to help. It doesn't matter if you don't wish to hear my woes, I'm telling you, anyway!

Ah, the sweetest of life. What is the point? As strange as it is wonderful, as bitter as it is sweet. Life is to feel and to hold, to laugh and to cry, to enjoy the strains of its music, the fading of the days light. It is everything we make it to be. For me, life is writing. It's who I am. It's what makes me happy.

"Life, happy or unhappy, successful or unsuccessful, is extraordinarily interesting," says George Bernard Shaw. I like that. I think I'll just keep on keeping on...

The last page(s)

Who said, "The end is always inevitable." I did!
C. Hawkins

The last two pages. Believe it or not, I've run out of things to talk about.

"I can't think of anything more to write for this book, and I don't have a proper ending," I complained to my husband one night.

"You, at a loss for words! That's amazing," he said, "considering you can spend an hour talking on the phone about nothing or stand in line at the supermarket and know everyone in it before you leave, not to mention the hours you spend e-mailing your friends."

Writing is different. What do you say when there's nothing more to say? I guess I could rattle on about nothing, but it would probably end up becoming idle gossip. Think about all the idle gossip we already hear in the world, most of which goes in one ear and out the other--at least it should. Even as Christians we spend a lot of time murmuring about one thing or another. Ephesians 4:25 says, "Let each of you speak the truth to your neighbor." There's a lot of wasted energy in idle gossip. Nothing good ever comes of it.

As a child I was very opinionated. (Some say I haven't changed much, that I'm still very outspoken). My blatant honesty often hurts people's feelings and sometimes, more than not, gets me into a heap of trouble. I've learned over the years to temper my opinions, to curb my tongue.

Example: If your friend asks you if you like her new hat and you really hate it. You don't have to say, "I really hate that hat." Instead, you could say, "That's a nice color on you." In otherwords, find something good to say about that hat. Temper your words, but still speak the truth.

I suppose tempering one's true feelings is necessary, sometimes, but I'm not sure it's a good thing. The Bible urges us to always tell the truth. Jesus had strong words for those who stood in the way of truth. If we strive to be like Jesus, doesn't that mean we will be tellers of the truth? Or in my case, a teller of stories. It's what I do best, and you have to admit, I do keep you entertained.

If this book seems a bit short to you, lacking in substance--truth is, I have nothing further to say, for now, and that's the truth!

This book is finally at an end. In spite of the editing efforts of some good friends, you may find a few mistakes here and there--I'd like to have you think we made them on purpose--just to fill your hearts with joy.

Thanks for buying a copy, my friend. Hope you enjoyed reading *Sailing Through Life*...**as much as I enjoyed writing it.**
Until next time, *fondly, Connie*

End